Sue Ellen

EDITH FISHER HUNTER

Illustrated by Bea Holmes

1969
HOUGHTON MIFFLIN COMPANY BOSTON

E964715

jH 9169 su

Also by
Edith Fisher Hunter

Child of the Silent Night

CONTENTS

1

Sleepy Sue Ellen

THE CLASSROOM was empty now, except for Sue Ellen. Everyone else had gone out for after-lunch recess. Mrs. Perry had gone to the teachers' room for a little while. She didn't know that Sue Ellen hadn't gone out with the others.

Sue Ellen tiptoed over to the wastebasket. She had seen Betsy Hall throw her brown lunch bag away before she'd gone out to play. Most of the other children had left their lunch bags and boxes on the floor.

Sue Ellen was hungry! She took Betsy's bag out of the basket and opened it. She looked in among the crumpled sandwich bags. As usual, Betsy had left one whole sandwich untouched. Although it was a little squashed, it was still in its plastic bag. Sue Ellen took it out and separated the two pieces of bread. She wanted to see what kind of a sandwich it was. Chicken! Big pieces of chicken. Sue Ellen loved chicken. She gobbled up the sandwich — all but the crust.

She was still hungry. She looked in Betsy's bag again.

This time she found three cookies. There were little pieces of chocolate all through the cookies. They tasted good! Betsy hadn't eaten her apple either, so Sue Ellen ate that too. Then she crumpled up Betsy's bag and threw it back into the wastebasket.

Through the open window Sue Ellen could hear the children on the playground screaming and yelling. She walked over by the big window. Sue Ellen was so little that she had to pull herself up on her elbows and lie on her tummy on the window sill to see outside. Now she could see the older boys playing baseball out in the back field near the woods. She couldn't see her big brother, Henry, but she knew he was out there playing.

Sue Ellen could see her big sister, Victoria. She and a crowd of her friends were chasing a gang of boys around the jungle gym. Lots of the children were on the jungle gym, and on the swings, and on the slide. Near the driveway some of the boys were playing marbles in the dirt, and most of the girls from her room were playing jump rope with Betsy Hall's long rope.

> *Rin-tin-tin*
> *Swallowed a pin*
> *He went to the doctor*
> *And the doctor wasn't in.*

Sue Ellen could hear the girls chanting while Betsy jumped. It looked like fun. Sue Ellen sighed. She

guessed she wouldn't go out, though. The swings were all taken and there was a long line waiting at the slide. She couldn't swing Betsy's heavy rope the way she was supposed to so they wouldn't let her play jump rope with them.

The June sun was streaming in the open window on Sue Ellen's head and shoulders. It felt nice and warm. Now that she had enough food in her stomach she felt comfortable, and sleepy. She slipped back down off the window sill and went over to the far corner of the room to the very end of the row of coat hooks. Perhaps Mrs. Perry wouldn't notice her there. She curled herself up in a tight ball on the floor, pulled her blue sweater snugly around her, and in just a few minutes Sue Ellen was fast asleep.

Mrs. Perry and Mrs. Garvey, the principal, had stopped by the door of Mrs. Perry's room to talk for a few minutes. The bell had not rung yet for the end of recess.

"Oh dear," said Mrs. Perry. "Just look at my room! Lunch boxes and paper bags on the floor, and someone's sweater left lying in a heap. I must get after my children as soon as they come in." Mrs. Perry had a reputation for keeping the neatest classroom in the Morristown Center School. "A place for everything and everything in its place," she often told her children.

Mrs. Garvey was looking at the dirty blue sweater on the floor. A pair of shabby shoes that had come unstitched at both toes was poking out from beneath it. "That's not *just* a sweater, Mrs. Perry," said Mrs. Garvey, slowly. "That's Sue Ellen Stokley curled up asleep."

"That child!" exclaimed Mrs. Perry. "Why doesn't she do her sleeping at home? In all my years of teaching, I've never had such a sleeper as Sue Ellen. The twins didn't fall asleep in school the way she does."

"No," said Mrs. Garvey. "Things were a little better for the Stokleys then. But they've had nothing but sickness and a stream of babies since Sue Ellen was born."

"Henry and Victoria weren't geniuses by any means," continued Mrs. Perry, "but at least I was able to teach them both to read. Here it is the end of the year, and Sue Ellen isn't even ready to read. Why, it's all I can do to keep track of where that child is! I've been tempted at times to tie her in her seat."

"Well, for one thing," observed Mrs. Garvey, "she doesn't get enough to eat. It's hard to believe that she's almost eight years old. She looks no bigger than a five-year-old, and even then she's nothing but skin and bones. A hungry child can't concentrate on school work."

"That's true," agreed Mrs. Perry. "She probably stayed in today so she could finish up Betsy Hall's lunch. I've found her doing it more than once."

"Perhaps things will be better for little Sue Ellen next year," said Mrs. Garvey. "I wanted to tell you that I've put her name down for the special new class that is being organized for the fall. It will be made up of children like Sue Ellen who have learning problems. This class will meet in Parkville and include youngsters from all the towns around here. Sue Ellen was the only child I suggested from our school."

As Mrs. Garvey finished speaking, the bell rang for the end of recess and she went on down the hall to her office. In another minute a noise like wild elephants charging could be heard coming from the other direction. Loud as it was, the noise did not wake Sue Ellen.

Quickly Mrs. Perry hurried out into the hall and held up her hand. The sound of wild elephants stopped as suddenly as it had begun. The children stood motionless, just as if they were playing a game of statues. They did not make a sound. Everyone in Mrs. Perry's room knew that when their teacher raised her hand like that they were supposed to stop whatever they were doing and listen.

Mrs. Perry walked quietly toward her class. She began to speak very seriously, separating each word as she said it. "That — was — a — very — noisy — entrance — children." She paused. Then she let just the suggestion of a smile cross her face. "I suppose I must expect it with summer vacation coming." A little ripple of relieved laughter began to sweep across the group. Up went Mrs. Perry's hand again. Silence again.

"Now," said Mrs. Perry, "let's see if we can go the rest of the way more quietly."

As usual, Tommy Stroud was at the head of the line. He was the biggest boy in the class. When he wanted to be first in a line, everybody let him. As soon as he was inside the room he rushed over to hang up his cap. He noticed the blue sweater, with feet, lying near his hook.

"Mrs. Perry," shouted Tommy. "Sue Ellen's asleep again. Want me to wake her up for you?"

"No, thank you, Tommy. I'll do the waking up. I want you to get the broom and sweep this end of the room. George and Glen, give me those marbles, please. I don't want to have to listen to them roll around your desks all afternoon. Just remember to ask me for them before you go home. Whoever has left a lunch box or paper bag or anything else on the floor, please pick it up and put it where it belongs. When Mrs. Garvey came by our room after lunch, I was ashamed!"

Everyone set right to work while Mrs. Perry went over to wake up Sue Ellen. "Come on, child. Time for school work again. You've napped long enough." Mrs. Perry had to shake Sue Ellen several times before she woke up. Then the teacher went back to her desk.

Sue Ellen sat up. At first she couldn't figure out where she was. She rubbed her eyes to get them open wide enough to look around and then she heard Mrs. Perry call Betsy Hall up to her desk. Now Sue Ellen knew that she was at school. She wished that she could lie down again and go back to sleep, but she didn't dare. And anyway, Tommy Stroud was trying to sweep right where she was sitting. He kept running his broom into her back.

Sue Ellen got up and started toward her desk, still rubbing her eyes. She bumped into Betsy Hall coming down the aisle carrying an important looking envelope. Betsy was always doing errands for the teacher. Then Sue Ellen heard her own name being called. She wondered what Mrs. Perry wanted. She wished she were being asked to do an errand for the teacher like Betsy Hall, but she knew she wasn't. Mrs. Perry never asked her to do errands. Probably the teacher was going to scold her for not going out to play with the other children.

Just as Sue Ellen reached Mrs. Perry's desk, the toe of one of her torn shoes caught on the floor and Sue Ellen landed head first in the teacher's lap.

Mrs. Perry sighed and helped Sue Ellen up. "Not quite awake yet, Sue Ellen? Why don't you go down to the girls' room and wash your face and hands? It ought to help you wake up and then perhaps you'll do your work better. See if you can smooth your hair up, too. It's all mussy from being slept on."

Sue Ellen turned and started back down the aisle. She scuffed her feet along the floor as she went so her torn shoes couldn't trip her up again. As she passed Tommy Stroud's desk, she heard Mrs. Perry tell the class to take out their music books. And she heard Tommy Stroud whisper, loud enough for everyone around his desk to hear: "Do we have to sing those same junky songs again?" Mrs. Perry's class always had music right after lunch, and they almost always sang the same songs every day.

Sue Ellen closed the door of Mrs. Perry's room behind her carefully. There was no one in the long hall ahead of her. Quickly she kicked off her two shoes and watched them go slithering down the length of the hall all by themselves. Then she skipped along after them in her stocking feet.

Sue Ellen would take a long, long time to wash up. She might even find a corner somewhere and go back to sleep again. After a while Mrs. Perry would probably send Betsy Hall down to find out why she was taking so long. It might be almost time to go home before Sue Ellen got back to Mrs. Perry's room.

2

Sue Ellen Stays on the Bus

Sue ELLEN had an empty feeling at the bottom of her stomach. She wanted the bus to hurry up and come, and she didn't want it to come — ever. Mostly she didn't want it to come.

It was the first day of school again. Sue Ellen and Henry were standing in the road outside the dilapidated green house where they lived. It was a little square house with a woodshed tacked on the rear. Mr. Stokley had hammered two boards over the pane of broken glass in the front door. There were no front steps so everyone used the back door. The shingles were broken across the front of the house where Henry played ball against them.

In the dirt around the house lay an assortment of old toys: a naked doll without any head, truck cabs without any bodies, a battered tricycle, and a wagon with one wheel missing. Behind the house at the edge of the woods was the outhouse that the Stokleys used instead of an indoor bathroom. At one side of the house there were some fallen-down chicken houses and the cellar hole of a barn that had burned down several years ago.

Sue Ellen and Henry were standing across the street from the house waiting for the school bus. They had been ready and waiting for a long time. All of the little Stokleys were out in the road playing and waiting with them. The bus was supposed to get to their house, the first stop on the route, at half-past seven.

Already the sun was warm. It was going to be a hot day for September. Sue Ellen decided to take her sweater off and leave it at home. It was torn under one arm and it was too small anyway. Her dress was too big, but it was the best one she could find to put on. Sue Ellen ran across the road and threw her sweater toward the house. It landed in the dirt on top of the headless doll.

At last, way down the road by Carlsons' farm Sue Ellen saw the bus come around the bend. Her heart began to beat hard. Mr. Carlson's old collie dog, Sandy, was chasing the bus, barking wildly, snapping at the huge tires. Sandy would be out in the road barking at the bus every morning and every afternoon from now on.

"Here she comes," shouted Henry, excitedly. "Barbara, get the kids out of the road. Hurry up, Scott, go on. You don't want to get hit do you? Barbara, get Martha. Quick, get her out of the way. Mr. Washing-

ton will be turning the bus around." The Stokleys lived
two miles out on a dead end road. The driver always
took the bus to the end of the road, swung it around,
and then came back to pick up the children.

Sue Ellen's brother Henry was a terrible worrier.
He worried about the whole family, all six of them;
eight if you counted Ma and Pa, and there were times
when Sue Ellen thought he worried more about them
than about the kids. Too much worry and not enough
food had made Henry skinny and nervous. He blinked
his eyes all the time. The school nurse, Mrs. Carboni,
said he had a tic.

"That Victoria is going to miss the bus for sure! Go
get her, Sue Ellen," fretted Henry. The bus was coming back now.

Before Sue Ellen could do anything, the back door
of the Stokleys' house opened, and Victoria came flying
out. Mr. Washington, the bus driver, knew what to expect. He stopped the bus while Victoria crossed the
street in front of him. Sue Ellen knew it would be like
this all year long. Victoria would just make the bus
every single morning. She'd never be ready ahead of
time, but she'd never miss it, either.

Mr. Washington reached over and pulled the lever
that opened the bus doors.

"Hello, kids. All ready for another year?"

"Hi, Mr. Washington," said Victoria, getting on the

bus first. Although she was the last one out of the house, she was usually the first one to get on the bus. Everyone said the twins were certainly different. Henry worried about everyone in the family. Victoria worried only about Victoria. Sue Ellen got on the bus second and Henry got on last.

Henry followed Victoria down the aisle to the back of the bus. He and Victoria always rode in the last seat because they got the most bumps there. Sue Ellen always sat in the first seat behind Mr. Washington. She didn't like the bumps. They made her feel sick to her stomach.

Henry and Victoria had been riding together on the back seat of the bus ever since they started going to school six years ago. Henry had to stay back this year so he was going into the fifth grade again. Victoria was going into the sixth.

Mr. Washington didn't start the bus up immediately. He waited a minute with the doors open. He looked out his open window toward the little green house where Barbara, Scott, and Martha were standing in a row in front of the broken shingles.

"No new customers this year?" called out the driver. "Nobody else coming?" It was a foolish question. The children's faces were dirty, their clothes ragged, and all three of them were barefoot.

"Me not going," shouted Scott, boldly. Barbara and

Martha, looking wide-eyed and frightened, backed up as close to the house as possible and shook their heads at the driver.

Sue Ellen wondered whether she ought to say anything, but then Henry called from the back of the bus. "They ain't goin', Mr. Washington. Barbara don't start school until next year."

"Then whose turn will it be?" asked the driver, looking at Henry in the long mirror over his head.

"Scott's," said Henry, "and then in a couple of years Martha gets to go."

"I guess I'll have to keep on driving this bus for a good many more years to get all you Stokleys through school," said Mr. Washington. "Then I'll turn the job over to you, Henry. OK?"

"OK," agreed Henry, although Sue Ellen couldn't imagine her brother with a whole bus load of children to worry about!

Mr. Washington pulled the lever that closed the doors, shifted into gear, and the bus started down the road. Sue Ellen waved out of her window to Barbara, Scott, and Martha. They all waved back.

Sue Ellen was thinking as she rode along. It would be nice when Barbara started going to school. Barbara could sit with her in the front seat. Sue Ellen didn't like the way it was now — sitting alone, waiting and waiting and hoping that someone would choose the seat next to her. Lots of times no one did. She knew why, too. Tommy Stroud called her "Smelly-Sue-Elly."

As the bus passed Carlsons' farm, Sandy came out to bark again. Then he turned around twice and lay down in the middle of the road to take his morning nap on the warm tar in the sun. Sue Ellen knew that the old dog would be all right there. No one used the road much. The electric company truck and Briggs's oil truck were just about the only cars that ever came up to Stokleys'. Ma let the kids play in the road all the time. She didn't worry about them out there.

But they all knew she'd lick them if they went down by the pond alone. The bus was passing the pond now. Sometimes Ma let Henry take all the kids down there to catch frogs. Sue Ellen was the best at catching frogs. She was the quickest. She used to wade right into the water up to her knees to catch them.

But not any more. Not after Henry saw the snapping turtle. After that she didn't dare wade in any more. Henry said that if the turtle got hold of her toe he wouldn't let go. He might even bite it off. She was sorry the ugly old thing lived in the pond. He'd spoiled her fun. The pond still looked pretty from far away but when she got close to it she thought she saw the snaky head of the turtle sticking up out of the water.

Sue Ellen gave a little shiver. For some reason,

thinking about the pond and the snapper made her think about school and about the first day of school last year. Ma had been sick in bed that day so Henry had helped Sue Ellen get ready. She never wore shoes in the summer and Henry hadn't thought of shoes for her until the last minute. The big box under Ma's bed had lots of shoes in it, but they were all mixed in together. Henry had finally found two that matched and fitted her, but they didn't have any laces. He found some laces in another pair, pulled them out and got them into her shoes just in time. He tied them up for her on the bus. Sue Ellen still couldn't tie her own shoe laces.

When the bus had arrived at school on that first day last year, Victoria hurried off and disappeared. Henry took Sue Ellen to Mrs. Perry's room and left her. She was so frightened after he'd gone that she hid in the hall. But Mrs. Perry found her and made her sit at a desk. Sue Ellen didn't stay there though. Every time Mrs. Perry turned her back, Sue Ellen got up and hid again.

Sue Ellen didn't want to think about what happened after that. Everyone moved so fast and talked so fast it made her dizzy. She couldn't understand the way people talked and they couldn't understand the way she talked. She didn't know anything about numbers or letters. She couldn't even tell which were which.

At first Mrs. Perry thought Sue Ellen couldn't see,

but even after Mrs. Carboni took her to get glasses, she
couldn't see what other people saw. She'd lost her
glasses long ago. Mrs. Perry thought that perhaps Sue
Ellen was deaf too, but she wasn't deaf. She just wasn't
used to having people talk to her. They didn't talk to
each other much at her house. Mostly she tried to stay
out of her father and mother's way. If she bothered
them, they were more apt to hit her than to talk to her.
If she didn't bother them, they usually left her alone.

As Sue Ellen rode along in the bus she decided that
she wouldn't think about last year at school any more.
But it was just as frightening to think about this year!
What was going to happen today when the bus reached
the Center school? Ma had told her not to get off.
Why? She'd gotten off last year. All the little kids
were supposed to get off at the Center school. Why
shouldn't she?

It made Sue Ellen sick to think about it. Well, she
wouldn't think about it. She'd just look out the window.

The bus was stopping at Petrys' dairy farm. This
was where her father worked. Sue Ellen could see his
old car parked in the yard. He was somewhere out
back in the barn. The two big Petry boys got on the
bus and went down back to sit with Henry and Victoria. Victoria made Henry move so Ralph Petry
could sit with her. She said Ralph was her boy friend.

The bus stopped again. This was Hardings' apple

farm. Three children were waiting for the bus; two boys and a girl. Sue Ellen could count to three, but after that she got mixed up. There was a woman waiting, too. That was Mrs. Harding. She was pretty. Last year only the two boys had ridden the bus. This was the first year that their little sister had been old enough for school. She had on a ruffly dress and fluffy sweater. Her hair was brushed into long curls that hung down around her neck.

The step up onto the bus was so high that Mrs. Harding had to help her little girl up. Sue Ellen could see that the little girl had been crying.

Mr. Washington spoke up. "Guess I'm taking your baby today, Mrs. Harding. Now you can go have yourself a good time."

Sue Ellen looked at Mrs. Harding. She looked ready to cry, too.

"Don't say that!" said Mrs. Harding, attempting to smile. "Good-bye, sweetheart. I'll be waiting for the bus." She stepped back as Mr. Washington closed the doors and drove away.

Sue Ellen was glad that the little girl had taken the seat next to her. The little girl didn't know that she was sitting next to the "Smelly-Sue-Elly" that her brothers joked about.

The houses were closer together now and the bus stopped more often. Lots of children got on at the trailer park, and at Spencer's store there was another large group waiting. The bus was a long way from Sue Ellen's house now. She knew it was a long way because one day she and Henry had walked to this store. There had been no food in the house that day and Ma had given Henry money to get macaroni and milk. Henry had told Sue Ellen that she was a good sport to walk so far.

Several more children were waiting for the bus at the Four Corners. Sue Ellen knew most of them. Tommy Stroud was the first one to get on. He was bigger than ever.

"Back to jail!" announced Tommy in a loud, cheerful voice. "And this year the jailer is 'Crabby-Miss-Abby.' "

"Well," laughed Mr. Washington, "at least this jail gives vacations."

The little Harding girl looked ready to cry again.

When the last child had gotten on at the Four Corners the bus was nearly full. Sue Ellen knew there would be no more stops. Anyone who lived between the Four Corners and school had to walk. They weren't bus children.

There were more and more houses now, and many groups of children walking along the side of the road. The bus passed Betsy Hall's big house. Sue Ellen saw Betsy coming down the driveway. She was wearing a pretty new dress. Now the bus was going past the library, the gas station, the fire house, Jim's Store, and the church. Then Mr. Washington turned into the driveway that circled around behind the school.

Sue Ellen's heart was pounding. It was hard for her to breathe.

The bus stopped. The doors swung open. "All out for the Morristown Center School," called out Mr. Washington.

Sue Ellen didn't move. The little Harding girl looked at Sue Ellen and she didn't move either. Most of the other children started crowding down the aisle. All of the children who went to the first six grades were supposed to get off the bus here. The older pupils stayed on and rode over to Parkville to the high school.

The two Harding boys came down the aisle. "Come on, Sis," said the older boy. "We all get off here," and he took his sister's hand and helped her off the bus.

Still, Sue Ellen didn't move.

Mr. Washington was looking in the wide mirror over his head. He saw Sue Ellen sitting in the front seat behind him. "What are you waiting for, Sue Ellen, Christmas?" joked the driver. "This is your stop."

At that moment Henry arrived at the front of the bus. Of course Victoria had pushed her way off long ago. Henry began to speak to Mr. Washington in a low voice. "Sue Ellen's supposed to stay on the bus.

She's going to a special class in Parkville this year."

"Oh, that's right, Henry," said the driver. "Mrs. Garvey told me that but I forgot. Thanks for reminding me." He looked up into the mirror, caught Sue Ellen's eye and smiled. "OK, Sue Ellen, my mistake."

Henry got off and went around the bus. As he passed Sue Ellen's window he smiled and waved. Sue Ellen felt like crying. She was used to having Henry nearby to take care of her. She wanted to be with him. What would happen if she got off the bus after all? Suddenly she made up her mind. She *would* get off. She started to get up.

"All aboard for Parkville," announced Mr. Washington. Sue Ellen had decided too late. She sat down again. The bus driver signaled to the big boys and girls who were waiting to get on. These were the high-school students who lived in town and rode the bus over to Parkville.

George Hall, Betsy's older brother, was the first to board the bus. He saw Sue Ellen sitting in the seat that he usually had. "Say, Sue Ellen, you'd better hurry up and get off. You may be smart but you aren't smart enough for high school yet!" Some of the older boys and girls who were already on the bus began to laugh. Sue Ellen sank down into her seat. She wished she could go on sinking right through the floor of the bus and never come up again.

A big girl was standing on the bus step directly behind George. She was waiting to get on. Sue Ellen didn't know her, but the girl knew Sue Ellen. Her name was Polly Smith. One Thanksgiving Polly and her mother had taken a basket of food and clothing to the Stokleys.

Quickly Polly stepped around George and sat down in the seat next to Sue Ellen. "Too bad, George," said Polly smiling sweetly up at him. "Sue Ellen and I are going to be sitting in these two seats this year."

Mr. Washington spoke up. "Polly's right, George. Sue Ellen is sitting just exactly where she belongs. You'll have to buy your tickets earlier next year."

George looked a bit mystified but shrugged his shoulders and went on down to the back of the bus.

As the rest of the high school boys and girls boarded the bus, Polly began to talk to Sue Ellen. "My name's Polly Smith. My mother teaches over in the high school. She told me about the new class you're going to be in this year."

Sue Ellen didn't say anything, but she smiled at Polly. She smiled because she had discovered that people were nicer to her usually if she smiled. Even when she didn't understand what they were talking about, she smiled.

Polly went on talking. "Mother met your teacher. Her name is Miss Kelly and mother says she's really nice. She has all kinds of surprises ready in your room. I think you're going to have fun."

Still Sue Ellen didn't say anything. She just kept on smiling. She wasn't quite as frightened now and her heart wasn't pounding as hard. But she did wonder what there could possibly be in a schoolroom that could make school fun. Last year, at the beginning of the year, Mrs. Perry had let the girls bring their dolls to school and the boys their little cars and trucks. But after a while Mrs. Perry had said that big boys and girls didn't need toys in school. She said that they should play at home and do their work at school.

Polly Smith began talking again. "Mother says she's never met a teacher like Miss Kelly. I'd like to meet her." Then Polly had an idea. "I know, Sue Ellen! How would you like to have me show you where your room is? It's across the street from the high school, over in the elementary school. I know which room it is too. I'll take you over so you don't get lost."

Sue Ellen smiled again.

3

A Special Class

Sue ELLEN and Polly were standing at the door of Miss Kelly's room, looking in. At least Polly was looking in. Sue Ellen was hiding behind Polly's skirt. She really didn't want to go into that strange room at all. She didn't know anyone in there. Perhaps she would slip away from Polly and hide somewhere.

"Oh look, Sue Ellen, tropical fish!" exclaimed Polly. "We have some like that at our house. And there's a turtle, too. Come on," and Polly started into the room.

At the mention of a turtle, Sue Ellen clutched Polly's skirt. But she did follow Polly into the room. The fish tank was on a low table near the door. She could see the turtle. Good! It was not a snapping turtle! It was just a tiny turtle with spots on its head. The turtle was sitting on a little raft that was floating on top of the water. When Sue Ellen and Polly came closer to the tank the turtle dove into the water. It nearly bumped into a fish that was swimming past.

Suddenly Sue Ellen heard a faint squeaking sound. She wondered if it had come from the fish tank. Then she heard it again! Beyond the tank on a shelf Sue Ellen saw two wooden boxes. They were just alike. There were screens on the tops of them and little bottles tipped on their sides above the screens. She decided to find out whether the squeaking noise was coming from one of the boxes. She pulled Polly along with her.

Sue Ellen looked down into the first box. All she could see were little pieces of wood. "Ain't nothin' in there."

Polly was looking more carefully. "Yes, there is. See the tiny ball of black fur in the wood chips? That's a mouse. I had a mouse for a pet once."

A mouse! Sue Ellen hated mice. Sometimes they ran across the kitchen floor and Ma made Henry whack at them with the broom. Henry had never been quick enough to hit one. "Where's him at?" whispered Sue Ellen.

Polly pointed to the black mouse in a corner of the cage almost buried in the chips. Its sides were quivering as it looked up at the girls out of beady little eyes. Then it squeaked again. "Hi, you squeaker," laughed Polly.

Still clutching Polly's skirt, Sue Ellen looked in the second box. This time she knew what to look for and she saw another mouse curled up asleep.

"I guess one is a boy and the other is a girl," said Polly, noticing a sign with the word "HE" on one cage and a sign with the word "SHE" on the other. Sue Ellen wondered how Polly knew one was a girl and the other was a boy.

As the two girls stood looking at the mice, a loud hammering started up. It seemed to be coming from a little room that opened off the large room in which they were standing.

"This place is certainly full of surprises," said Polly, leading the way into the small room. Two boys were standing in front of a long work bench. One of the boys had a hammer in his hand. He was trying to hit a nail that was part way into a piece of wood. When he hammered, he hit the wood instead of the nail.

"Watch me, Patrick," shouted the boy with the hammer. "I'm making something," and he went on hammering noisily.

Sue Ellen let go of Polly's skirt and put both hands over her ears. She hated loud noises. But she was thinking how much Henry would like a room like this. He was always trying to make things. On the wall behind the work bench hung all kinds of tools and on the floor there was a huge box full of wood.

Polly saw that Sue Ellen had covered her ears so she turned to leave the noisy little room. As they got beyond the sound of the hammering Polly said, "The boys

will have fun in there, won't they? Don't you love the
smell of freshly cut wood? I do."

Sue Ellen didn't know whether or not she liked the
smell in that room, but she did know that Miss Kelly's
room was a lot different from Mrs. Perry's room. The
part they had come to now looked like a kitchen. There
was a refrigerator, a shiny white stove, and in the corner
a sink and an ironing board. On the wall behind the
stove there was a peg board covered with cooking utensils. There were shelves of dishes and boxes of silver-
ware and a big kitchen table.

"This looks like my mother's room over in the high
school," said Polly. "She teaches Home Ec; that's
cooking and sewing and things like that. Your class is
lucky, Sue Ellen. Most of us don't have Home Ec and
Shop until junior high."

In the space beyond the kitchen corner there were
three long shelves filled with real groceries. Behind
the shelves on the wall hung huge signs with letters and
numbers that Sue Ellen couldn't read. At the end of
the shelves there was a high table with a toy cash register on it, and parked beside the table a grocery cart.
Sue Ellen thought this part of the room looked like
Spencer's grocery store.

Polly must have thought so, too. She said, "This
must be the store where you'll buy the food you're going
to cook."

Sue Ellen wondered how she would like cooking. She had never cooked anything in her life. Since Pa had thrown out the old black wood stove, Ma just had a hot plate to cook on. She wouldn't let anyone touch it except Pa and Henry. She didn't want anyone to get hurt.

A girl, just a little taller than Sue Ellen, was standing near the cash register. She was looking down at the floor. Sue Ellen wondered what she was looking at. She didn't look up at Sue Ellen or Polly as they walked by. Even when Polly said, "Hi," she didn't look up or answer. She didn't do anything. She just stood there staring at the floor.

Beyond the cash register the room became a still different kind of place. Here there were low shelves stacked with blocks and small cars and trucks. In the corner there was a pretty rug on the floor. Two dolls were sitting at a table set with dolls' dishes. Another doll was lying in a cradle. Sue Ellen wished her sister Barbara could see all this. She loved to play with dolls.

Near the doll corner a tall, thin girl was looking through a big box filled to overflowing with grown-up people's clothes. There were dresses and hats, pocketbooks and high-heeled shoes. The tall girl was trying on some of the things. Polly said, "Hi," to her, too. The girl hesitated a minute, and then she smiled and said, "H-h-hi."

"This room looks as if it would be much more fun than high school," said Polly. "I think I'll just stay here today."

Sue Ellen was happy. She thought Polly really meant she was going to stay with her. She was glad. She skipped ahead and looked in the door of another little room. There was a cot with a bright colored cover on it and beyond that a toilet and a little box place. Sue Ellen didn't know what that was. She'd never seen a shower stall.

At last the girls came to the final section of the big room. This part, Sue Ellen thought, really did look like a school room. There was one big desk and then a lot of smaller desks and chairs. There was a blackboard with shelves of books under it. Another long shelf held piles of paper, boxes of scissors, jars of paint, cans of brushes, and boxes of crayons. In Mrs. Perry's room these things were kept in Mrs. Perry's locked supply closet. No one could go in there unless Mrs. Perry gave them the key.

Near the teacher's desk there was a table with a type-writer on it. Mrs. Garvey had a typewriter in her office in the Center School. Once, when Sue Ellen was in the office waiting to see the school nurse and Mrs. Garvey wasn't there, she had pushed down on the long thing across the front. It had jumped. Sue Ellen thought she'd broken it. This was probably the teacher's typewriter, Sue Ellen decided.

"Oh, look," exclaimed Polly, "loops for making potholders! I love to make potholders. And I see some wooden puzzles, and just look at the games — checkers and dominoes, and lotto. Honestly, Sue Ellen, this room is just like home. It isn't like school at all."

Sue Ellen smiled, although she couldn't understand why Polly thought the room was like home. It wasn't like her home. But she was glad Polly liked it and was going to stay with her.

Up near the teacher's desk two women were talking. Sue Ellen suddenly felt afraid again and caught hold of Polly's skirt. Polly knew one of the women. Her name was Mrs. Briggs. She was a friend of Polly's mother. The other woman was short and plump with soft curly white hair and rosy cheeks. She was wearing a flowered smock. Polly decided she must be Miss Kelly, the teacher.

She had her arm around a rather fat little girl. That was Jenny Briggs. Polly knew about her. Jenny had been injured when she was born and she had trouble remembering things. She had never been to school, but Polly's mother had told Polly that because of the special new class Jenny was going to try going to school. If she enjoyed it and if the teacher felt it was worthwhile, Jenny would be going for half a day.

Sue Ellen decided to hide behind Polly again. She heard one lady say, "Thank you, Miss Kelly." Then she heard the other lady say: "Jenny and I have a lot to do this morning, Mrs. Briggs, so please don't come back too soon." The lady named Mrs. Briggs nodded, waved good-bye, and left the room.

Polly walked right up to Miss Kelly. Sue Ellen came along behind her. "Good morning," said Polly. "My name is Polly Smith and I'd like you to meet Sue Ellen Stokley. She's going to be in your room this year. We rode over on the bus together from Morristown and I thought I'd help her find your room."

"That was nice of you, Polly," said Miss Kelly pleasantly. "I had trouble finding it the first day myself."

Miss Kelly reached around Polly and took both of Sue Ellen's hands in hers. "I noticed you two girls exploring our room and I decided that you must be Sue Ellen. Mrs. Perry told me that you were quite short, and that you had big blue eyes, yellow hair, and a friendly smile."

Sue Ellen looked timidly up at her new teacher. She liked the way this teacher talked to her. Although she was still frightened, she managed to smile.

"It's nearly time for classes, Polly," said Miss Kelly. "You'd better run. Thank you ever so much for helping Sue Ellen find the way."

"I just love your room, Miss Kelly," said Polly enthusiastically. "I wish I could stay! Good-bye, Sue Ellen. I'll see you after school on the bus," and Polly started to leave.

"Ain't you going to stay?" asked Sue Ellen in a frightened whisper. "You said you was going to stay. Don't leave me here alone."

"Why don't you come by and pick Sue Ellen up after school, Polly?" suggested Miss Kelly. "Then she'll be sure to get on the right bus. Sue Ellen will be ready to tell you all about our room then. Run along now, Polly, so you won't be late."

Miss Kelly led Sue Ellen over toward two of the desks. "I want you to meet Jenny Briggs, Sue Ellen. You and Jenny are going to sit next to each other this year. This desk will be Jenny's and this one will be yours." As Miss Kelly finished speaking the bell rang for school to begin and Polly disappeared out the door.

Sue Ellen sat down beside Jenny. Only she and Jenny were sitting at their desks and there were still only a few other children anywhere in the big room.

Miss Kelly had gone over to speak to the little girl who had been standing by the cash register. She was still standing there. When Miss Kelly spoke to her, she did not look up. She did not move. Even when the teacher put her arm around her, she didn't budge. Sue Ellen began to worry. Maybe Miss Kelly would take her by the shoulder and march her right over to her desk. That's what Mrs. Perry used to do to her when she wouldn't sit down.

But Miss Kelly did nothing of the sort. She just smiled, gave the little girl a pat on the shoulder, and walked over to speak to the tall, thin girl who was playing in the doll corner. When Miss Kelly spoke to her she immediately started to take off the lady's hat and high-heeled shoes that she was wearing. Then she hurried over and sat down at one of the desks.

The two boys who were in the woodworking room came out when Miss Kelly asked them to. The boy named Patrick was given the desk behind Sue Ellen. He sat right down and folded his hands in front of him on the desk. He didn't say anything.

The other boy was as noisy as Patrick was quiet. He was the one who had been hammering. Although he came over to his desk when Miss Kelly asked him to, he would not sit down at it. Miss Kelly called him Tod. She said that it would be all right if he didn't sit down, just as long as he knew where his desk was and where his things were to be kept. She asked him to stand near his desk for a few minutes while she talked to the class.

Behind the two boys there were two more desks. The tall girl was sitting at one of them. She had her hand up and was waving it back and forth.

"Yes, Ruth?" said Miss Kelly.

"Wh-wh-who go-gar nog, whgn-." She was getting

her words all twisted up. She couldn't seem to get them out in the right order. When she tried to hurry, she sounded even worse.

Sue Ellen wondered if Miss Kelly would yell at the girl? Would she tell her to stop and think? No, Miss Kelly waited patiently. Once she suggested quietly that Ruth try to start over again more slowly. Ruth tried, but after a minute she began stuttering again.

Miss Kelly must have decided that Ruth had tried long enough. She seemed to know what it was that Ruth wanted to ask anyway.

"You would like to know who is going to sit beside you this year, Ruth? Your desk mate will be Sheri Stafford." Miss Kelly nodded in the direction of the little girl who was still standing near the cash register staring at the floor. "When Sheri feels at home enough to enjoy being with us, she'll sit at the desk beside you. Then there will be Sue Ellen Stokley and Jenny Briggs; Tod Swan and Patrick O'Neil; Sheri Stafford and Ruth Wood."

Sue Ellen was wondering. Were these all the children who were ever going to be in Miss Kelly's room? It was such a big room and there were more desks, all empty, on the other side of the aisle beyond Sue Ellen's desk. Wasn't anyone going to be sitting at those desks?

Miss Kelly was speaking again. "Tomorrow the rest of our class will come to school. Since I'm new this year and since you children are new to each other, I thought it would be best if just you six younger children came today. Tomorrow the six older children will join us. When we're all here, there will be twelve in our class."

Jenny had already gotten up from her desk. She had gone over to look at the fish. Then she went into the woodworking room. Then she went over to the store and started piling things in the shopping cart. Miss Kelly was watching her, but she didn't say anything.

Tod, the noisy boy, had decided that he didn't want to stand by his desk any longer. He had gone over to the block shelf and had made a tall tower of blocks. Then he took a small truck and started to drive it straight at the tower. He was making a noise that sounded exactly like a truck motor. When the truck hit the blocks, the tower went over with a crash. Tod laughed and laughed.

Again Sue Ellen waited for Miss Kelly to do something. But she didn't. She went on talking quietly to the three children who were still sitting at their desks. Patrick was looking out the window. He was smiling, but he wasn't smiling at anyone. When Miss Kelly asked him a question, he didn't seem to hear her. It was as if he had gone away from himself and wasn't there to answer. Sue Ellen thought surely Miss Kelly would tell him to pay attention. But she didn't.

Ruth was sitting with her head on her desk. Her desk was near the fish tank, and she was watching the fish swim back and forth, back and forth. She was humming softly to herself. Sue Ellen was still sitting at her desk. She thought she might get up and go over with Jenny in a minute. She wasn't listening to Miss Kelly.

She was thinking. This room certainly was not at all like Mrs. Perry's room, and Miss Kelly was certainly not like Mrs. Perry. Sue Ellen thought she might almost like going to school in this room. But in the back of her mind, she was a little worried. She remembered that Mrs. Perry had said school was a place to do your work and that playing should be done at home. Sue Ellen liked to play. She could play in this room. But Sue Ellen really and truly wanted to be able to read. Her father could not read at all. She didn't want to grow up and not be able to read. But learning to read was hard work. Sue Ellen wondered whether she could learn to read in this nice room.

4

A No-School Day

THIS WAS a no-school day. Sue Ellen lay in bed wishing it was a school day. This year she wished that every day was a school day. But wishing wouldn't change it. This was a no-school day and the next day would be too. Then there would be school again.

Barbara was still asleep in bed beside her. It didn't matter to Barbara that there was no school. She didn't go to school. She didn't go anywhere. Sue Ellen could remember how it had been before she started going to school. Every day had been just the same as every other day. Except that on some days there was less to eat, and on some days her mother was sicker than on other days.

Victoria was still asleep, too. She had her own bed at the foot of Barbara and Sue Ellen's bed. She wouldn't sleep with anyone else. She said she didn't want anyone getting her bed all wet. Henry and Scott slept in another bed by the window. Two round humps under the blankets showed that the boys were still asleep. A third hump showed that Whiker, the cat, was still asleep, too. Really his name was Whiskers, but Scott couldn't say his "s's" so he called the cat Whiker, and now everyone else did, too.

Sue Ellen could hear her mother and the baby in the kitchen. Her father had gone to work long ago. For a minute Sue Ellen thought about her father. He left early in the morning while it was still dark. He worked every single day at Petrys' dairy farm. They said they didn't want him if he wouldn't work every day. They said that the cows have to be milked every day — two times a day. Cows don't know about no-school days or Christmas or anything. So he went to work every day. Sometimes he got home right after the second milking. When he came in he made the whole house smell like cows. If he was tired everyone had to go to bed as soon as he'd finished eating. He said he had to have his sleep if he was going to earn money for them all.

But sometimes he didn't come right home. On those days he drove over to Parkville and he didn't come back until late at night. When he finally got home he was noisy and everyone was careful to stay out of his way. On those nights no one got much sleep. It was after noisy nights that Sue Ellen usually took a long nap at school on the cot in the little room. Miss Kelly didn't mind. She said that was what the cot was there for. She said that no one could do school work without a good night's sleep and a full stomach, and if Sue Ellen couldn't get enough sleep and enough to eat at home, she'd have to get them at school.

Sue Ellen's father had come home very late last night. Even then he hadn't gone to bed but turned the TV on loud. He said he didn't care if all the kids stayed up and watched just as long as they didn't bother him. So everybody watched the late show. Martha and Scott and Barbara had finally fallen asleep in a heap on the floor. That was the reason everyone was still asleep; all except Pa and Ma and the baby.

Sue Ellen decided not to get up yet. There really wasn't anything to get up for. She'd just lie in bed and think about school. Henry said they'd been going to school now for a month. That meant a long time. Every day she liked school better. If Sue Ellen kept her eyes closed, she could see her room at school and her teacher wearing one of her pretty smocks.

Miss Kelly was nice. All the kids liked her. She had made up new names for them all. Sue Ellen giggled as she thought of some of the names. Miss Kelly called Patrick, "Handsome"; and Tod, "Mr. Right Hand Man"; and Jenny, "Lady Helpful"; and Sue Ellen, "Miss Busy." Every morning as the class arrived at school, Miss Kelly had something nice to say to each one of them. She didn't hurry them and tell them to get right to work either. She said it took her a little while to get used to school in the morning and she guessed they probably felt the same way.

Miss Kelly always let Sue Ellen say hello to her friends and visit with the mice — Sue Ellen dared to hold a mouse now — and to see how the fish were. Then Miss Kelly would remind her to go in and wash her face and hands, brush her teeth, and comb her hair. Everyone in Miss Kelly's class had a washcloth, a towel, a toothbrush, and a comb at school. Miss Kelly had shown everyone how to do a good job using them.

Sue Ellen liked to run the hot water until the basin was nearly full. They didn't have hot water at her house, and anyway she couldn't get near the kitchen sink to wash even with the cold water before the bus came. Her mother needed to use the sink, or Victoria was busy fixing her hair.

Sue Ellen liked the smell of the soap that Miss Kelly had for them at school. Miss Kelly said it was pine, like the pine tree in the school yard. Sue Ellen took a long time getting her hands soapy. Sometimes all she did was play with the soap and not really wash at all. Then she had to go back and start over again. Once a week she took a shower and if her clothes were very dirty or her socks had big holes in them, Miss Kelly looked in a special closet and found something else for Sue Ellen to put on. Miss Kelly had explained to her class one day that each of the children in her room

needed special kinds of extra help. That was why they were in her room. Some of them needed special help with their reading, some with their number work, some with how to talk better, some with how to sit still and listen, some with their feelings, and some with being clean and healthy. Miss Kelly said she needed extra help too. She needed help in learning how to be a good special class teacher, and this class was helping her to learn.

Usually by the time Sue Ellen had finished washing, the rest of the class was sitting around the two big tables eating. Anyone who was hungry could have milk and cereal. Sometimes there was toast and jam, too. After that the class would sit and talk and plan for a little while. Miss Kelly said people ought to take time to have a little fun in life and sitting around a table eating and talking and planning what they were going to do each day was fun.

No one ever sat around a table to eat or talk at Sue Ellen's house. There weren't enough chairs for everyone and they didn't all eat at the same time anyway. Most of the time, if someone said they were hungry and if there was anything in the house to eat, Ma gave them something and told them to run on outside with it.

Just thinking about breakfast at school made Sue Ellen hungry as she lay in bed at home. Ma was yelling

at the baby now. Suddenly there was a loud slap and
the baby started crying.

Sue Ellen could guess what had happened. Martha
wanted to go out and play in the road. Probably Ma
was tired of saying no and had slapped her. She
wouldn't let the baby go out alone. Lots of times Sue
Ellen had heard her mother say that she'd brought all
these children into the world and she wasn't going to
have anything happen to any one of them. For a long
time she'd been able to keep the baby in her crib all day,
but now Martha could climb out over the side. She did,
too! Once she'd slipped out the shed door and gone half
way to Carlsons' all by herself before Henry had found
her. Now Ma tied the shed door shut.

Sue Ellen could hear the baby crying softly. She
knew how her little sister looked, sitting with her back
against the door holding her sweater and sucking her
thumb. Even though she couldn't talk, Martha knew
how to let people know what she wanted. When she
wanted to go out, she'd get her sweater and stand or sit
by the door.

Martha really wasn't a baby any more. Sue Ellen
didn't know how old she was but she wasn't a baby. But
all the Stokleys called her the baby. Probably if the
baby that had been born after Martha hadn't been born
dead, they would have stopped calling Martha "baby."

Sue Ellen sighed, thinking about it. Ever since that
baby her mother had been sick and cross. Some days
she couldn't even get out of bed. She almost never did
any washing or cleaning up around the place any more.
Henry did most of the cooking that got done.

Suddenly Sue Ellen decided to get up. The sun was
out. She could see it shining under the blanket that Ma
hung across the window by the boys' bed to keep out the
light. Maybe it would be nice and warm outside. It
had gotten so cold last night that Ma had asked Henry
to help her light the oil heater. Now the house was too
hot.

Without waking up Barbara, Sue Ellen crawled out
her side of the bed. She pulled on the dress that was
lying on the floor and slipped her feet into some shoes.
Then she went into the kitchen with Whiker following
her.

"Get that baby out of here, Sue Ellen," said her
mother. "She's been whining to go out for an hour.
Here's a piece of bread for the both of you. And don't
you dare go near the pond. I'm going to lie down 'til
the rest of them gets up. I don't feel too good."

Sue Ellen put Martha's sweater on her. She knew
how to dress the baby. She'd been taking care of her
little brother and sisters ever since she could remember.
She found her own blue sweater under the kitchen table
and put it on. Then she and Martha went out into the

shed. Sue Ellen slipped the string off the doorknob and they went down the back steps together.

It was nice outside. The sun was out. It wasn't warm, but it wasn't cold, either. Sue Ellen decided to walk to the end of the road and up into the field. Martha loved to go for walks but she walked queerly. She always looked as if she were going to tip over. Mrs. Carboni said it was because she had been kept in her crib too long and hadn't had the right food to eat.

Sue Ellen gave Martha half the piece of bread as they started out. The road was covered with nuts that had fallen from the big tree just beyond the house. They were the kind of nuts that have little saucers on the bottom. A squirrel was sitting on his haunches in the middle of the road, holding one of the nuts between his paws. Martha saw him. She picked up a nut and threw it at the squirrel. She was a good thrower because she and Scott and Barbara spent so much time playing in the road throwing stones. The nut rolled up to where the squirrel was sitting. Surprised, he looked at the two little girls. Then he ran over to the tree and scrambled up it. The little girls laughed as they watched the squirrel disappear among the branches.

The leaves of the trees were all different colors. Sue Ellen knew the names of the colors now: red, orange, yellow, green, and blue. But she still got mixed up trying to decide which name went with which color; except for blue and red. She knew those two. The sky was blue and fire engines were red. She knew those because Miss Kelly had let each person in the class who didn't know his colors point to the color that he liked best. Then she pinned a ribbon of that color on the clothes of each person.

Sue Ellen's favorite color was blue. Her sweater was blue. Her eyes were blue. Martha's eyes were blue too. She knew red because red was Jenny's favorite color and Jenny's ribbon was red. The leaves on some of the trees were red and so were the leaves that covered the stone wall.

"Look," whispered Sue Ellen, reaching for Martha's little hand. The two children stood still as a dark, furry animal about as large as a cat humped his way across the road directly in front of them. He waddled up onto the top of the stone wall and disappeared between two big boulders.

"Him's a woodchuck, Martha," explained Sue Ellen. "Mr. Carlson's dog kills woodchucks. Him grabs their necks and shakes them dead. I ain't scared of them," added Sue Ellen bravely, although she knew she really was.

The road came to an end just ahead of the girls. "Let's go up and pick some flowers," suggested Sue Ellen. She found the narrow path that led into the field. Mr. Stokley used the field as a dump. The children walked past parts of a crib, the old iron stove, some broken bed springs, rotted-out mattresses, and the rusty body of a car. Beyond the dumped things, the field became pretty again. No one hayed up here any more and the tall grass and wild flowers were blowing together all across the field. Sue Ellen did not know the names of any of the flowers, but she thought they were pretty. Ma liked flowers too. She always put the flowers they brought home to her in a glass of water on the kitchen table.

"Let's sit down," said Sue Ellen, and she helped Martha find a place to sit in the deep grass. Martha laughed as the grass tickled her neck. Sue Ellen liked to hear her little sister laugh. "That's grass," Sue Ellen explained, "and that's sky," she added, pointing up over her head. "Sky's blue. I love blue."

Martha didn't say anything, but she smiled and looked up in the direction Sue Ellen was pointing. It frightened Sue Ellen a little when she looked at Martha. Even though her little sister played out of doors most of the time she looked very pale. Already Martha had been taken to the hospital three times with what Ma called "fainting spells." Once Sue Ellen had heard Mrs. Carlson ask Henry if Martha was "just right." Henry had said he didn't know, but he guessed she was. It had worried Sue Ellen to hear Mrs. Carlson ask

Henry that question. She wished her little sister could
have some of the milk and cereal and toast that she was
having in Miss Kelly's room at school this year. But it
would be a long time before Martha would be old
enough to go to school.

Sue Ellen put her arms around Martha and gave her
a tight hug. She loved her little sister and she had decided something this morning while she was lying in
bed. That was why she had gotten out of bed so suddenly. She had decided that she was going to be
Martha's special teacher at home, just the way Miss
Kelly was her special teacher at school.

She had decided this because of something Miss
Kelly had told the class one day. Sue Ellen couldn't
remember it all, but the point was that she wanted the
boys and girls in her class to be special teachers to their
little brothers and sisters at home. She explained that
it's hard to learn things if no one talks to you or does
things with you when you're little. Miss Kelly said that
she realized that many of their fathers and mothers had
to work very hard and didn't have much time. But the
children in her class had time and they could teach
their little brothers and sisters just the way she was
teaching them.

Sue Ellen had not forgotten that conversation. She
had decided that of the kids at home, Martha needed
a special teacher most. Barbara and Scott had each

other, but Martha couldn't even talk yet. Ma didn't feel well enough to talk to her or do things with her, so Sue Ellen would have to.

"Hear them birds?" said Sue Ellen, pointing to a tree loaded with whistling, cackling starlings. "Them's going away when it gets cold. Miss Kelly said so."

In the distance, Sue Ellen heard the sound of Mr. Briggs's oil truck coming up the road, and then she heard the Carlson's dog Sandy begin to bark. The birds were frightened by the barking. They rose up from the branches of the tree, circled once overhead, and then swung off into the blue sky.

"Bye-bye birds," said Sue Ellen. "Wave bye-bye, Martha." She took her sister's fragile little hand in hers and helped her wave good-bye to the birds who were going away to keep warm.

5

How Many Are Coming?

SUE ELLEN'S class had been getting ready for Hallow-e'en. They had been planning a party to be held in their own room at school. They were going to cook lunch themselves and they had sent out invitations to some of the special friends of their class. After lunch they were going to play Hallowe'en games. For days and days they had been cutting out paper pumpkins and witches and cats to hang around the room.

Sue Ellen had felt a little sick to her stomach on the way to school this morning because she was so excited about the party. Then, when Polly got on the bus, Sue Ellen found out that the party was not today after all, but the day after today. Sue Ellen had just learned the word for the day after today — tomorrow. Polly said the party was tomorrow, Thursday, and this was only Wednesday. Polly was coming to the party.

Sue Ellen didn't know the names of the days of the week yet. Miss Kelly was trying to help her learn them.

Before this year Sue Ellen had never really cared about the names of the days. Nothing special ever happened to her, so what difference did it make what day it was? But now that Sue Ellen looked forward to going to school, and now that special things were happening almost every week, Sue Ellen had discovered that she needed to know the names of the days so she could keep them straight in her mind. She felt the same way about telling time now, too. She was beginning to want to know what time it was so that she could know how soon some fun thing was going to happen. But Sue Ellen couldn't tell time at all, yet.

Miss Kelly's class was sitting around the two big tables having their morning snack. They were going over the final plans for tomorrow's party. In Mrs. Perry's room, Betsy Hall's mother and Mrs. Perry planned the parties. But in Miss Kelly's room, everyone helped do the planning, and then everyone had jobs to do for the party. Sue Ellen was discovering what a lot of work there is to giving a party. So far there had been two birthday parties. Sue Ellen had never had a birthday party, but this year she was going to have one. Everyone in Miss Kelly's class would have a birthday party.

No one was absent today. Sue Ellen looked around at all her friends. Jenny, Tod, Patrick, Sheri, Ruth, and Sue Ellen were sitting at the table with Miss Kelly. The older children were sitting around the long work table with Miss Foster. Miss Foster was going to be a teacher like Miss Kelly someday, and she was learning to teach by helping in Miss Kelly's room.

As the children ate they were talking about who was going to come to their party. "We've invited Jenny's mother," said Miss Kelly.

"My mummy will help us cook," said Jenny, jumping up from her chair. "I'll be at the party, too. But my daddy won't come. He has to work." Jenny looked at Miss Kelly, and then, as if she had just remembered something, Jenny went back and sat down in her chair again.

Miss Kelly was trying to help the children in her class learn that at morning snack time everyone sat around the tables and talked and planned. It was not a time to be getting up and down. Sue Ellen knew that sometimes Miss Kelly called Jenny, Tod, and her the three jumping jacks.

The teacher smiled as she watched Jenny remember to sit down. She said, "That's right, Jenny, we certainly couldn't have the party without your mother. She'll be in early to help us cook tomorrow. I'm so glad I found out what a good cook she is!"

"We've invited Mrs. Winter, too," said Miss Foster. "She's certainly a real friend to this class."

Sue Ellen liked Mrs. Winter. Her children were all grown up. She said she missed them and so she came in sometimes in the afternoon to play games with the children in Miss Kelly's class. She played checkers, and dominoes, and crazy eights, and lotto. She said she used to play all those games with her own children. Sue Ellen wondered what it would be like to have a mother who liked to cook, like Jenny's mother, or one who liked to sit down and play games with her children, like Mrs. Winter.

Yesterday when Mrs. Winter came in she had brought pumpkins from her garden. The boys carried them in from her car and Sue Ellen and Jenny and Mrs. Winter counted them. There were twelve pumpkins and twelve children in the class. Then they played store. David, one of the big boys, was the storekeeper. There were scales in the store now and David helped each person pick out a pumpkin, weigh it, and then pay for it with real money. The pumpkins cost one cent a pound. Sue Ellen's pumpkin weighed five pounds and cost five cents.

"Sue Ellen," Miss Kelly was speaking to her now. "Go over and stand at the bottom of our number line, and we'll figure out together exactly how many people are going to be at our party. We need to know so we can set the right number of places."

On the floor in the middle of the room a ladder of great big numbers from 0 to 10 had been painted. Sue Ellen went over and stood on the big zero. Her two feet just fitted inside the circle. She didn't know what Miss Kelly wanted her to do next.

"Jenny," said Miss Kelly, "I want you to count the people at our two tables. Ruth, will you please go over and stand near Sue Ellen. Make sure she goes up just one number any time Jenny counts another person." Although Ruth stuttered and had a difficult time talking, she was good at number work.

Sue Ellen was glad Miss Kelly had asked Ruth to stand near her. Now she wouldn't worry about whether or not she was doing it right. When she worried she usually did things wrong.

"Sheri," said Miss Kelly, "will you go over to the blackboard and write down the numbers as Sue Ellen steps on them. Write great big huge numbers, Sheri, so we can all read them."

Sue Ellen liked Sheri a lot. Although she still said hardly anything, she no longer just stood looking at the floor. She was beginning to do things with the class and this week she had started sitting at the table with Sue Ellen at snack time. Miss Kelly had asked Sheri to write big numbers because usually when Sheri wrote anything it was so tiny no one could read what she had written.

"Now, Jenny," suggested Miss Kelly, "why don't you start counting with Tod and go right around the two tables until you come to me."

Jenny walked over and put her hand on Tod's shoulder. If no one interrupted her, Jenny could count very well. "One, two, three, four," Jenny counted. But then she tripped over the leg of David's chair. Jenny stopped her counting and stamped her foot. "You spoiled me, David; now I'll have to start all over again."

Jenny went back to Tod and started counting again. This worried Sue Ellen. What should she do now? Should she go back to the zero? Ruth whispered: "S-st-st-stay there, S-Sue Ellen. I'll-ll s-st-st-start you."

Jenny was beginning to count again. "One, two, three, four, five — ."

Ruth gave Sue Ellen a little push at the "five" and Sue Ellen began to move again.

"Six, seven, eight, nine, ten." Jenny put her hand on Miss Kelly's shoulder as she said "ten."

"That's fine, Jenny," said Miss Kelly, "and I see that Sue Ellen is where she should be on the ten, and Sheri is putting down her big number ten on the blackboard. Very good! Jenny, Ruth, and Sue Ellen, you may all sit down now. We'll still need you, Sheri."

Sue Ellen skipped happily back to her chair. Oh, how she loved this room! Miss Kelly didn't give her things to do that were too hard for her. And the other kids in the room really wanted to help her. It wasn't like Mrs. Perry's room where everyone always wanted to be the first one to get his hand up and the first one to say the answers. In Miss Kelly's room they were more like her brother, Henry. They all took care of each other.

Sue Ellen wished Henry could be in Miss Kelly's room this year. He was having a hard time even though he was doing the fifth grade over again. Sue Ellen knew why he was having a hard time, too. He worried too much. The more he worried, the more mistakes he made. The more mistakes he made, the more he worried. Somehow Miss Kelly helped you not to worry so much.

"Now," said Miss Kelly, "I'm going to ask Patrick to do the next counting for us. Jenny counted the ten people at the tables. But she didn't count the people who were standing up. She didn't count herself" — Miss Kelly held up one finger — "or Sheri, or Ruth, or Sue Ellen." Each time Miss Kelly named a person, she held up another finger. She had four fingers up. "What we want to know, Patrick, is how much are ten and four more?"

Patrick squinched up his eyes the way he did when he needed to do some hard thinking. If no one hurried him he often got the right answers. Sue Ellen hoped he was going to get the right answer now. She liked Patrick, but he was a worrier like Henry. Patrick's father had gone away one day and never come back.

Patrick talked about him a lot. He was waiting for him to come back and take him to the ball game like he said he was going to.

Patrick was still thinking, but he was shaking his head. He didn't know the answer. Sue Ellen didn't either.

"Give it a try, Patrick," said Miss Kelly.

But Patrick didn't want to make a mistake. Teachers yell at you when you make mistakes. Except Miss Kelly didn't. She said you can't learn without making mistakes. She said she'd made a million mistakes in her life.

But Sue Ellen knew how Patrick felt. Mrs. Perry used to yell, "Think, Sue Ellen," when she made a mistake, and then she couldn't think one bit.

Very patiently Miss Kelly held up one finger. "If Jenny makes one more than ten, how many do we have?"

"Eleven," whispered Patrick. He always whispered when he was nervous.

"Fine," said Miss Kelly. "Now we need one more and one more and one more."

Patrick was moving his lips. At last he whispered, "Fourteen."

"Good for you, Patrick," said Miss Kelly. "Ten and four more make fourteen."

Doreen, one of the older girls, had her hand raised.

"Yes, Doreen?" said Miss Kelly.

"We haven't counted Mrs. Briggs and Mrs. Winter, yet. Fourteen and two more are sixteen."

"Right," said Miss Kelly, "and we also sent an invitation to Polly Smith. That makes seventeen. Sheri, please write the numbers from ten to seventeen on the blackboard. Keep them nice and big."

Sue Ellen was glad Polly was coming to the party. Polly wanted to be a teacher someday, and she was coming in to help in Miss Kelly's room during her study hours.

"So, I guess we'll need to set seventeen places at our tables," said Miss Kelly.

But Sheri was busy writing one more number on the blackboard — a great big huge one and eight.

"Why did you put down that eighteen, Sheri?" asked Miss Kelly. "Polly made it just seventeen."

"Because we invited Father Tom, too," said Sheri.

"So we did," agreed Miss Kelly. "We want to have singing at our party, don't we?"

Father Tom worked at one of the churches in Parkville. He had a guitar. He came into Miss Kelly's room every week and sang with the class. When they sang with Father Tom, they sat on the floor or stood up if they wanted to. They didn't have music books. They didn't need them. They just learned the words as they went along. Sue Ellen knew all the words to Father

Tom's songs. She hadn't known the words of any of the songs in Mrs. Perry's room. Singing in Miss Kelly's room wasn't like singing in Mrs. Perry's room at all. She wondered if Tommy Stroud would think Father Tom's songs were "junky" too?

"Tod," said Miss Kelly, "look over at the blackboard and tell us how many people are coming to our party now."

Tod studied the great big one and eight for a minute and then he said, "Eighty-one."

Miss Kelly smiled. "I hope not! We'd run out of food! You've turned the numbers around, Tod. Lots of people make that mistake. Start reading with the *one*, not the *eight*."

Tod looked at the numbers again and then he said, "Eighteen."

"Right," said Miss Kelly. "Now, Miss Foster, I would like you to work with the older children using the numbers that Sheri has written on the blackboard. Let them do some addition and subtraction. For example, they might figure out how many people will be at our party if Father Tom can't come or if someone in the class is sick."

"I won't be sick," burst in Jenny, "and my mummy won't be sick."

"No, I'm sure you won't," laughed Miss Kelly. "Run get your coat on, Jenny. I'm going to take you and Sue

Ellen and Patrick and Tod and Sheri and Ruth on some errands around town. There are several things we still need for our party."

Slowly Sue Ellen followed Jenny out into the hall to get her jacket. She didn't like to have Miss Kelly even suggest that someone might be sick and miss the Hallowe'en party. That would be the worst thing that could happen to anyone.

6

All Around the Town

SUE ELLEN was trying to pull her jacket on over her head. The zipper was stuck near the top and she couldn't quite squeeze her head through the opening. Below the zipper, the jacket was all undone and the lining was torn and hanging down.

Miss Kelly saw Sue Ellen struggling with her jacket. "Come here, Sue Ellen, and let me see if I can move that zipper down. The rest of you do up your jackets. It's pretty nippy outside."

The teacher took Sue Ellen's jacket and worked on the zipper. She was finally able to pull it down far enough so that Sue Ellen could slip her head through. "Better leave it unzipped so you can take it off when we get back," cautioned Miss Kelly.

As she gave the jacket back to Sue Ellen she noticed Tod and Jenny chasing each other up and down the hall. "Tod and Jenny, come over here and calm down. When we go down town on errands, you have to act more grown up than that."

Miss Kelly began to study the list she had taken out
of her pocket. "Our first stop will be the bank. We
can't do much without money."

Sue Ellen knew that was true. Usually her mother
didn't have money and couldn't buy anything. Her
father kept their money. He got it from Mr. Petry.
Sue Ellen's father didn't put his money in the bank. He
put it in his pants pocket. He liked to have a lot of
money in his pocket, although it didn't stay there long.

Miss Kelly had explained to her class that she had
been given one hundred dollars at the beginning of the
year. It was for her to use with her class for special
things. So far she had bought the groceries for their
store, the mice, the tropical fish and the wood scraps.
She also kept five dollars in the cash register for the
class to use when they played store. The rest of the
money Miss Kelly had put in the bank. She had shown
the children the check book that they had given her at
the bank. Whenever she wanted to use some of the
money, she wrote a check and the people at the bank
took that amount of money out of the class account.

Sue Ellen liked going down town with Miss Kelly.
She had never been shopping before she came to school
in Parkville. Pa did all their shopping. Sometimes
Victoria and Henry got to go, but no one else. It made
Sue Ellen feel important to go in and out of the stores
with Miss Kelly.

When the class reached the first crossing, Miss Kelly asked Jenny what color the sign at the side of the street was. Jenny knew because it was her favorite color, red. Then Miss Kelly asked Tod to read the sign. He started to read "POTS." but he caught himself just in time. He turned it around and read "STOP." Miss Kelly asked Patrick to read the next sign. It took Patrick a few minutes to sound it out, but he finally read, "CROSS HERE."

The children crossed the street and continued along the sidewalk until they came to the bank. They had been to the bank to cash a check once before. Outside the bank, Miss Kelly asked Sue Ellen a question. "Can you tell me the name of the first letter on the sign over the door?"

Sue Ellen looked up at the sign. Yes, she knew that one. "P," said Sue Ellen quickly.

"Good," said Miss Kelly. "That sign says 'Parkville Bank.' Parkville begins with 'P.'"

Sue Ellen was learning the names and the sounds of the different letters. She had discovered that the typewriter in Miss Kelly's room was not for the teacher to use, but was for the children in the class. Using the typewriter, Sue Ellen had learned the names of all the letters in just a few days. How surprised she was when she found out that all typewriters jump when you press down on the space bar or the letters. She hadn't broken

Mrs. Garvey's typewriter that day after all!

As the children stood outside the bank, Miss Kelly reminded them of something. "This is a place where people come on serious business. We have serious business to attend to, also."

The children walked quietly into the bank. They waited very nicely while Miss Kelly was getting their money. A woman worker beckoned to Jenny to come over to her desk. She gave Jenny six lollipops. There were very few people in the bank so early in the morning so Miss Kelly got the money quickly. She showed the children the five one-dollar bills she had been given for the five dollar check she had written.

Outside the bank Jenny handed each of the children a lollipop. Sue Ellen's was grape flavored. She liked grape. Each of the children carefully put their lollipop paper in the trash can on the sidewalk. That was what they had done when they had come to the bank before.

"We don't want to be little bugs," explained Jenny. "My mummy doesn't want me to be one. Tod, don't be a little bug. Put your paper in the trash can." Sue Ellen knew that Jenny meant "litterbug."

Miss Kelly was studying her shopping list again. "Our next stop will be Mr. Carter's printing shop. I want to find out if he has any more orange and black scrap paper that we can have to make our table decorations."

Mr. Carter was another good friend of the children in Miss Kelly's class. From time to time he sent over boxes of scrap paper for them to use. Today when they went into the shop Mr. Carter was sitting at his desk in the front office.

"Hi, Mr. Carter," said Tod. "It's us."

"Hi, Tod," said Mr. Carter. "This is just the crowd I was hoping to see. I was looking for something special to do with all that orange and black paper that we trimmed off the high school Hallowe'en dance posters and programs."

"Orange and black paper is exactly what we came in here for," said Miss Kelly.

"Want to come to our party, Mr. Carter?" asked Jenny. "He could come couldn't he, Miss Kelly? He wouldn't eat much." Jenny liked everyone and she enjoyed making other people feel happy. Sue Ellen wished that she was as brave as Jenny and dared talk to big people the way Jenny did.

"We'd be glad to have you, Mr. Carter," said Miss Kelly, "and you could eat all you wanted to. Can you come to lunch tomorrow? We're going to cook it ourselves."

"I'm afraid not," said Mr. Carter, "I'm too busy to

take much time off for lunch but it's nice to be invited. Come on out back and we'll get the paper. I'll show you kids why a printer has so much scrap paper to give away."

The class started out into the back shop. It was very noisy out there. "Slap-slap-slap" went one of the big machines. "Slap-slap-slap."

"That's a printing press," shouted Mr. Carter, "and so's that." They were walking past a second machine that was going "slap-slap-slap." Sue Ellen didn't like all the noise. Neither did Sheri or Patrick. They stayed close to Miss Kelly. Jenny and Ruth put their hands over their ears and Tod giggled and danced up and down as he walked along.

One of the men who worked for Mr. Carter was standing in front of another big machine. It had a flat table-like top on which there were several tall piles of paper arranged in a row.

"That's my new cutter," shouted Mr. Carter over the noise of all the machinery. "Stand back against the wall and watch what happens when Hank presses the button and turns the long bar."

The children crowded back against the wall and watched. When Hank pressed the button the machine began to make a loud noise. Sue Ellen thought it sounded like the school janitor's vacuum cleaner. When Hank put his two hands on the long bar, there was a whooshing sound and down came a knife blade and sliced off one side of the piles of paper. Hank swept the strips of paper that had been cut off into an enormous barrel that stood next to the cutter.

"That's where all the scrap paper comes from," shouted Mr. Carter. "Come on, now. Over here are the two boxes of orange and black paper. Patrick and Tod can manage them I'm sure. Let's go."

Sue Ellen was glad to get out of the noisy shop. In the front office they thanked Mr. Carter for the paper and started to leave.

"Wait, wait!" exclaimed Tod. "We forgot to pay. Where's our money, Miss Kelly?"

"Oh, no," said Mr. Carter. "I ought to pay you for taking away those trimmings. Save your money for food at your party. Then Jenny won't have to tell anyone else not to eat too much. Good-bye, kids. I'll expect to see you all again around Thanksgiving."

Outside the Carter Press, Miss Kelly looked at her list again. "Next stop is the dime store. We'll get our Hallowe'en napkins and the candles for our tables there."

By the time they reached the dime store they all had finished their lollipops. Jenny made certain that they all threw their lollipop sticks in the trash barrel outside the store. "We don't want to be little bugs, Miss Kelly, do we?"

"No, indeed," agreed Miss Kelly, smiling. "No little bugs in my class. Let's window shop for a few minutes before we go inside."

"Wh-wh-what's w-window sh-shopping?" asked Ruth. She loved pretty things but because she had seven brothers and sisters and no father at home there wasn't much money to buy them.

"Window shopping," explained Miss Kelly, "is looking at things in store windows and deciding what you'd like to buy if you had a million dollars. Really, you don't buy anything at all. It's lots of fun and absolutely free."

Sue Ellen thought it would be fun, too. She'd never heard of window shopping. She started to choose things in the window that she would like. The dime store window was all fixed up with Hallowe'en decorations. There were bright orange cardboard jack-o'-lanterns, black and white skeletons, and all kinds of Hallowe'en costumes with masks for faces.

"I'd like to have that witch costume," said Miss Kelly. "I think teachers make good witches."

"I don't like that one there," said Jenny, pointing to a boy's costume that consisted of black pantaloons, a red silky blouse, and a mask with a patch over one eye and a mean looking face. "He scares me. He isn't nice," said Jenny.

"That's a pirate," said Miss Kelly. "Pirates really

weren't very nice. Which costume would you like to have, Sue Ellen?"

Sue Ellen knew exactly which one she wanted. She pointed to a silky black cat costume. The mask that went with it had green and gold eyes and gold whiskers.

"If I'm a witch you can be my cat," said Miss Kelly, smiling and putting her arm around Sue Ellen. "Witches always have black cats and brooms. You could ride on my broom."

"I'm going to have the bones one," said Tod, getting very excited as he pointed at a skeleton costume. Suddenly he shaped his hands like claws and held them up in front of his face. He looked around for someone to scare. "I'm a monster," he said, showing his teeth and making his eyes all poppy. He put his claw-like hands right up in Sheri's face. Sheri moved over close to Sue Ellen to get away from him.

"Don't be afraid," said Jenny, stepping between Tod and Sheri. "Stop it right now, Tod. You shouldn't scare Sheri. She's very nervous." Jenny had heard her mother say that Sheri was nervous.

Tod grinned and stopped being a monster. "I wouldn't hurt you, Sheri. I'm sorry."

"Of course you wouldn't, Tod," said Miss Kelly. "Sheri's your friend. I want the rest of you children to think about what kind of a costume you would like for Hallowe'en. I forgot to tell you that Mrs. Winter is

coming in this afternoon with a big box full of Hallow-
e'en costumes. They were up in her attic and she said
she's sure there's one to fit everyone in our class."

Sue Ellen was excited when she heard that. Perhaps
she really would be able to have a black cat costume for
Hallowe'en. Betsy Hall had worn one in the Hallow-
e'en parade at the Center School last year. Sue Ellen
hadn't had a costume last year, but Mrs. Perry had
some extra torn sheets and she had fixed one into a costume for Sue Ellen. She had been a ghost. But more
than anything else this year Sue Ellen wanted to be a
black cat.

When the class had finished window shopping they
went into the dime store. They bought orange and
black candles and orange and black Hallowe'en napkins. The napkins had pictures on them of jack-o'-lan-
terns and of witches with black cats flying through the
air on brooms.

The last stop on Miss Kelly's list was the supermar-
ket. As they walked in the door Bill, the vegetable man,
saw them. He called out, "Hello, Miss Kelly and her
one-two-three-four-five-six children."

Sue Ellen liked Bill. She laughed when he called
them Miss Kelly's children. He always had something
funny to say when they came in.

Jenny went over and took one of the carts from the
row of empty grocery carts.

"Good," said Miss Kelly. "You know your job, don't you, Jenny? Tod and Patrick, why don't you put your boxes of paper on the bottom shelf of the cart while we shop?" She looked at her list again. "We need lettuce and tomatoes for salad. Tod, will you please pick out a head of lettuce and tell me how much it costs."

Tod picked out a cabbage by mistake. Bill showed him how much thicker and more slippery cabbage leaves feel than lettuce leaves. Then Bill showed him which sign gave the price of lettuce.

Tod studied it for a minute and said: "Ninety-two cents."

"Careful, Tod," warned Miss Kelly. "You've turned the numbers around again."

"Twenty-nine cents," said Tod, correcting himself.

"That's right," said Miss Kelly. "Sheri, will you pick out eight nice tomatoes, please? Bill will put them in a bag and weigh them for us. He'll tell us how much they weigh and how much each pound costs."

Sue Ellen watched Sheri pick out the eight tomatoes. She wished that they tasted as good as they looked. Sue Ellen did not like tomatoes. They never ate things like lettuce and tomatoes at her house.

When Sheri had chosen eight tomatoes, Bill weighed them and told Sheri that they weighed two pounds. He told her that each pound cost fifteen cents. Only Ruth could figure out that the two pounds cost thirty cents.

"Now we need a bag of potatoes," said Miss Kelly. "The older girls are going to make mashed potatoes to-morrow. Sue Ellen, will you put one of the smaller bags in our cart, please? They cost sixty-nine cents a bag." Sue Ellen put the bag of potatoes in the cart, but she wished they were going to have potato chips at the party instead of mashed potatoes. She liked chips better.

At the meat counter Miss Kelly asked Ruth to order three pounds of hamburger. Mr. Trent, the meat man, told Ruth that there was a good buy in hamburger at seventy-nine cents a pound.

"I w-wish it c-costed eighty," said Ruth. "I c-could d-do three eighties easy, b-but the n-nines are hard to add."

"I know," agreed Miss Kelly. "When we get back to school, Ruth, I'll show you a way to change most of the nines into tens and you'll be able to add up our whole grocery bill quite easily."

"This cart is getting heavy to push," complained Jenny. "Shopping makes me so tired!" She leaned her head against Miss Kelly.

"I'll help push," said Sue Ellen.

"Thank you," said Miss Kelly, "but I think we're all done. We have ketchup and mayonnaise at school. Mrs. Winter is bringing rolls, and we have cake mixes in our own store."

"What are we going to drink?" asked Todd. He was looking longingly toward the soft drinks on a nearby shelf. Sue Ellen hoped they were going to buy some, too. She and Tod loved sweet things.

"We'll have our regular milk and Kool-Aid," said Miss Kelly. "We have those at school. So if you'll push the cart to the check-out counter, girls, Mrs. Cook can add everything up for us."

After Miss Kelly had paid the bill she showed the children that she had just forty-five cents left from the five dollars with which they had started out. Later they would try to figure out together how much they had spent during the morning.

On the way back to school, Miss Kelly carried the bag of potatoes; Tod and Patrick carried the boxes of Hallowe'en paper; Sheri carried the lettuce and to-matoes; Ruth carried the hamburger; Jenny carried the paper napkins, and Sue Ellen carried the candles.

"This afternoon," Miss Kelly reminded them as they walked along, "Polly Smith will be in to help us cut our pumpkins into jack-o'-lanterns, and Mrs. Winter will be in with her box of costumes."

Sue Ellen couldn't help skipping as she went along. Oh, how she hoped there would be a black cat costume that fitted her in Mrs. Winter's box!

When the children arrived back at school they dis-covered that recess had begun and that Miss Foster and the older children were already out on the playground. Miss Kelly told her group to put their bundles on the table and run on out.

"All except Sue Ellen," said Miss Kelly. "I need to see Sue Ellen about something."

7

No Party for Sue Ellen—Almost

"Sue Ellen," said Miss Kelly. "I think I'd better take you in to see Mrs. Carboni. I want her to look at those sores on your neck. I noticed them when I was trying to fix the zipper on your jacket. They look to me as if they might be something catching."

Sue Ellen knew about her sores. They itched. She had been hoping they would go away but they hadn't. Instead they were getting worse. She knew that she had some on her back, too. As she followed Miss Kelly into the nurse's office she felt frightened. She wondered if Mrs. Carboni would have to do something to her that would hurt. She didn't like to be sick and she didn't like to be hurt.

When they arrived in the office, Mrs. Carboni was looking at a boy's knees. He had fallen off a swing and scraped both of his knees badly. He had gone right through his pants and his knees were bleeding and full of gravel. Sue Ellen had had plenty of scraped knees. She knew how they felt and she did not like to watch as the nurse cleaned him up and put on salve and bandages.

The next patient was a little girl who said she felt sick to her stomach. Mrs. Carboni took her temperature and then told her to lie down on the cot. She put a blanket over her and called up the little girl's mother. She asked her to come and take her home.

It was Sue Ellen's turn next. Mrs. Carboni examined the sores carefully. She loosened Sue Ellen's dress at the neck and of course she discovered the sores on her back.

"Sue Ellen," said Mrs. Carboni, sternly, "does anyone else have sores like these at home?"

Sue Ellen nodded her head. "Barbara and Martha got 'em."

"Well," said Mrs. Carboni, firmly, "you'll have to go right straight home and stay there until your skin clears up. We can't have other children catching this."

While Sue Ellen was doing up her dress, Miss Kelly reminded Mrs. Carboni that there was no one at the Stokleys' house who could come and get Sue Ellen.

"Let her sit down here then until I've finished," said the nurse. "I can drop her off on my way to the Center School." Mrs. Carboni was the nurse for all the schools around Parkville. She was a very busy person and had to hurry all the time.

Miss Kelly was not in a hurry. Somehow she always

seemed to have time to talk with children. She sat down
and drew Sue Ellen over close to her. Tears began to
spill out of Sue Ellen's eyes and roll down her thin
cheeks. Sue Ellen didn't know it, but Miss Kelly felt
like crying too.

"I'm sorry," said Miss Kelly. "I wish this hadn't
happened."

Sue Ellen nodded her head. She couldn't get her
voice around the lump in her throat to say anything.
The tears were running down her cheeks in two little
rivers.

Miss Kelly handed Sue Ellen a tissue from the pocket
of her smock. "I'll send Ruth over with your jacket and
some things for you to work on while you're out of
school. When Mrs. Carboni takes you home, she'll take
along enough medicine for you and Barbara and Martha. She'll explain to your mother how often to put it
on and you must be sure to remind her to do it. I don't
want you to miss any more school than is absolutely
necessary. I'm so proud of the work you're doing. Oh,
how I wish you didn't have to miss our party tomorrow!"

Sue Ellen nodded through her tears. The bell for
the end of recess rang and Miss Kelly had to go back
to her room. A few minutes later, Ruth appeared carrying Sue Ellen's jacket and a cardboard box.

"Too b-bad you're s-sick, S-Sue Ellen," said Ruth.

"Everyb-body's s-s-sorry." Sue Ellen knew that was true. No one in her room liked to have anything bad, like being sick, happen to anyone else.

After Ruth left, another boy with skinned knees arrived and Mrs. Carboni set to work on him. Sue Ellen did not want to watch. She decided to look in the box that Miss Kelly had sent over with Ruth. She found that there were two packages of crayons: one with all the colors, and one with just orange and black. Those were the Hallowe'en colors. She had learned them today.

The next things she found were a cardboard jack-o'-lantern, a cardboard witch on a broom, and a cardboard cat. Sue Ellen knew what she could do with those. Quickly she looked deeper in the box to see whether or not Miss Kelly had put in scissors, paper, and pencils. Yes, she had put in several pencils, two pairs of scissors, and lots of white, orange, and black paper. That was good. They didn't have things like that at her house. If Sue Ellen put the cardboard jack-o'-lantern on a piece of the paper she could draw around the edge of the pumpkin with a pencil. Then, if she cut along the pencil line she'd have two jack-o'-lanterns, the cardboard one and the paper one. That was how her class had made all the decorations for their party.

At the bottom of the box Sue Ellen found several reading work sheets. They were the kind Miss Foster had been helping her with. She was doing them so well that Miss Foster and Miss Kelly said she was going to be ready to read soon. That's why she was going to be especially careful not to lose the new glasses that Mrs. Carboni had gotten for her. But it was hard not to lose things at her house.

The mother of the little girl with the stomach ache had finally come to get her. "We can leave now, Sue Ellen," said Mrs. Carboni. "Hurry up because I'm supposed to be at the Center School by eleven. Pack up your box quickly and I'll run you home."

Sue Ellen did as she was told and followed Mrs. Carboni to her car. "Climb in back, please," said the nurse as she climbed in front. Sue Ellen tried to open the back door but the car was new and the door did not open the way the door on her father's old car opened. After Mrs. Carboni had gotten in she noticed that Sue Ellen was having trouble with the door. She reached around and opened it from the inside.

Mrs. Carboni drove very fast and in spite of all the curves and turns on the way to the Stokleys' they reached Sue Ellen's road quickly. As they passed Carlsons' farm, Sandy came running out to bark. He did not sleep in the road when the weather got cold.

But Scott, Barbara, and Martha were out playing just the same. They were in the road up beyond the house. Sue Ellen saw Scott riding around in circles on his battered tricycle. One of the back wheels was caved in so that it could only go in circles. Sue Ellen saw Scott stop to watch the unfamiliar car coming toward the house.

Barbara was trying to pull the rusty wagon with the missing wheel. Martha was sitting in the wagon gripping the sides tightly so she wouldn't fall out. Sue Ellen saw Barbara stop pulling the wagon and watch while Mrs. Carboni parked in front of the house.

Sue Ellen didn't even try to get out of the back seat. She had no idea which handle to use. There were several of them and even if she had known which one to use, she wouldn't have known whether to push it or pull it or turn it. So she just sat and waited until Mrs. Carboni noticed her and let her out.

"You stay out here and play, Sue Ellen. I want to talk to your mother and explain about the medicine. She can put it on you after I leave." Mrs. Carboni went around to the back door and knocked. Mrs. Stokley opened it almost immediately. She had seen the car pull up by the house. She knew the school nurse and let her in.

Mrs. Carboni didn't stay in the house very long. When she came out she told Sue Ellen she could take the other children inside and have the medicine put on. "But," said Mrs. Carboni, pointing at Barbara and Martha, "that medicine isn't going to do one bit of good

unless your mother cleans those children up." The
nurse climbed into her car and drove away quickly.

Sue Ellen took her two little sisters into the house
and their mother put the medicine on them. It didn't
hurt at all. Before Sue Ellen went to bed that night she
reminded her mother to put the medicine on them
again. Mr. Stokley came home very late and was noisy
and cross. His shouting woke Sue Ellen up and she
heard her mother crying. She hated to hear her mother
cry, so she buried her head under the blankets.

The next morning Sue Ellen was still in bed when
she heard Victoria yelling at her mother. Victoria had
put a lady's dress on the chair in the kitchen the night
before. It had come in a box of clothes that someone
had given to the Stokleys. Victoria was planning to
take it to school and wear it for a Hallowe'en costume.
When she couldn't find it she blamed her mother. Victoria was in her usual last-minute rush to catch the bus.
And, as usual, Henry was outside shouting for Victoria
to hurry up because the bus was coming. Victoria must
have found the dress because Sue Ellen heard the back
door slam and the bus start up and drive away.

It was the day for the Hallowe'en lunch party. Sue
Ellen had thought that nothing worse could happen to
anyone than to miss that party and now she was the one
who was going to miss it! She turned over in bed and
began to cry. She fell asleep again, crying.

When she woke up the second time, she heard her mother telling Scott and Barbara to stay outside and take care of Martha. "Me cold," Scott was shouting. He was pounding on the door. It was tied shut so he couldn't get in.

Mrs. Stokley came into the room where Sue Ellen was lying in bed. She rummaged around at the ends of several of the beds which were piled high with clothes. There were no closets in the Stokleys' house. The ends of the beds, the walls, and under the beds were the only places to keep things. Mrs. Stokley finally found a couple of sweaters and a jacket and went out into the shed.

Sue Ellen heard her mother open the door and say, "Here, put these on and run around. It ain't that cold." She heard Scott yell, "Me hungry." She heard him kick the bottom of the door. He was trying to push the door open before his mother could get the string back on.

"You already ate something," said his mother. "Go on! I don't want you in here now."

Sue Ellen could hear Martha crying outside. She decided to get up. If she didn't get up and have her mother put the medicine on her sores, they would never go away and she'd never get back to school.

Sue Ellen hurried to pull on a dress. She didn't bother with shoes. The oil heater was going full blast and the house was hot and stuffy. In the kitchen she stood on a chair and got the cereal box off the top of the refrigerator. She found a bowl in the sink and shook the last of the cereal into it. There wasn't much left.

Her mother had the TV going in her bedroom. Sue Ellen could see it from where she was sitting. That was funny! There was an ad on the TV for exactly the same kind of cereal as she was eating. In the ad a little boy was sitting at a table in a pretty kitchen. His mother was pouring cereal into his dish with one hand and with the other hand she was pouring in milk. Sue Ellen didn't have any milk on her cereal. Whenever her father came home late he forgot to bring milk, so there wasn't any milk this morning. Whiker, the cat, was rubbing his back against Sue Ellen's legs. He wanted some milk.

As Sue Ellen finished her cereal, she remembered about the medicine. "Ma," she called. "Ma." She had to shout over the television. "Did you put the medicine on Barbara and the baby?"

"No," said her mother. "They been out playin'."

"I'll get them in and wash them up," said Sue Ellen. "Then you can put it on all of us." Sue Ellen saw the tea-kettle sitting on the hot plate. "Could we have some hot water, Ma?" asked Sue Ellen.

"What do you need hot water for?" asked Mrs.

Stokley, crossly. She had grown up in the mountains where they didn't even have running water, never mind hot water. She didn't see why anyone needed to wash in hot water.

Sue Ellen knew that her mother didn't like anyone telling her how to run her house or how to take care of her family. But she just had to have that hot water. "Mrs. Carboni said the medicine ain't goin' to do no good if we're dirty. If I get hot water I can get the kids cleaner," explained Sue Ellen.

"Oh, all right, but don't you get them kids in here 'till the kettle's steamin'," said Mrs. Stokley. "I'll turn it on."

"And Ma," said Sue Ellen. Since her mother had agreed to the hot water perhaps she'd agree to something else. "Can I bring the kids into the bedroom? I'll play school with them. They won't bother you none."

"Oh, I suppose so," said Mrs. Stokley. Scott was kicking at the door again. The baby was crying. She sighed as she added: "If I didn't feel so bad all the time, Sue Ellen, I wouldn't mind having them kids underfoot. When winter comes I'll have to let them in here most all day long. I tell you, Sue Ellie, it ain't any fun feelin' sick all the time. It would be real nice if you'd play school with 'em."

Sue Ellen did a good job of getting herself and Barbara and Martha clean. She made sure that her mother put some of the medicine on every single sore spot, too. Then she made Scott and the two little girls stay in the kitchen until she got the beds smoothed up. There wasn't any space to play in the bedroom except on the beds. Miss Kelly was teaching the children in her class how to make a bed. Of course the Stokleys' beds didn't have sheets, but Sue Ellen could make the blankets lie quite flat. When she had finished she let the children in.

The cardboard box of school things was under Sue Ellen's bed. Scott was excited when he saw the scissors. He had never used scissors. But Sue Ellen wouldn't let him touch them until he'd traced something to cut out. She showed him how to trace around the jack-o'-lantern and then she showed him how to hold the scissors. But he used a different hand than she did — Miss Kelly called her a southpaw — so she couldn't help him very much. Sue Ellen showed Barbara how to trace around the cat. The witch on the broom would be hard. She'd do that one herself. She even gave little Martha a piece of paper and let her try to color with a black crayon. Martha made big scribble marks all over the paper.

Sue Ellen liked to play school. Sometimes when she played school she made believe that she was Mrs. Perry and then she yelled at the kids. But today she pre-

tended that she was Miss Kelly and she talked nicely to
her class and she sat down and did things with them,
the way Miss Kelly did.

The children were so busy that they didn't even hear
a car drive up and stop outside the house. Scott was the
one who finally heard the knocking at the shed door.
He hopped off the bed and ran to slip the string off
the doorknob. When the door opened, he let out a
yell. Everyone came running.

Someone was standing in the doorway wearing a
witch's mask and a black cape. Then, off came the
mask and there stood a smiling Mrs. Winter. She was
holding a jack-o'-lantern under one arm and a large
shopping bag in her other hand.

"Hi," laughed Mrs. Winter. "I hope I didn't scare
you, but Miss Kelly wanted Sue Ellen to see the costume that she is going to wear at the party this afternoon. She asked me to wear it when I brought over
your party, Sue Ellen."

Mrs. Winter introduced herself to Mrs. Stokley and
Mrs. Stokley invited her into the kitchen. First Mrs.
Winter handed the smiling jack-o'-lantern to Scott.
"That's the pumpkin Sue Ellen bought at our store
yesterday. Polly Smith carved it. There's a candle in-
side all ready to be lighted when it gets dark tonight."

Mrs. Winter began to rummage around in the shopping bag. When she found what she was looking for

she handed Sue Ellen a paper bag. "Here's your black cat costume. Miss Kelly said that was the one you wanted. Ruth and I figured out that it's just your size. I put in a couple of extra costumes, too. They were too small for anyone in the class and they just might fit Scott and Barbara."

Sue Ellen hugged the bag close to her. She couldn't believe that what was happening was real. Tonight they could all put on their costumes and go trick-or-treating up to the Carlsons'. Or maybe Pa would let them all pile in the old car and he'd drive them up to the Center like he did one year. There were lots of houses to trick-or-treat up there.

"Here's a box of Hallowe'en cupcakes," continued Mrs. Winter, still taking things out of her shopping bag. "Mrs. Briggs arrived at school with two dozen this morning. Everyone wanted you to have some, Sue Ellen." Mrs. Winter took the cover off the box and showed the children the jack-o'-lanterns made out of frosting on the top of each cake. Barbara took the box of cupcakes.

Mrs. Winter gave Martha a bag of candy corns to hold, and she handed Sue Ellen some of the Hallowe'en napkins that the class had bought at the dime store yesterday. The next package was a brown paper bag which Mrs. Winter handed to Mrs. Stokley. "Could these go in the coldest part of the refrigerator? They're

ice cream cups that Mr. Carter sent over. I guess he can't count, Sue Ellen, because he sent enough for three classes."

Finally Mrs. Winter reached into her shopping bag for the last time. She brought out a blue ski jacket with a hood to match. She held it up in front of Sue Ellen. "Miss Kelly said you were having trouble with the zipper on your other jacket. I think this one will fit you just fine. My goodness! Doesn't it make your eyes look blue!"

"Thank you, Mrs. Winter," said Sue Ellen, taking the jacket into her already loaded arms.

"You're welcome, Sue Ellen. Now I must hurry back to school and help get ready for the party there. It was certainly a beehive of activity when I left."

"We been playin' 'cool," burst in Scott. "Want me get what me done?" Without waiting for Mrs. Winter's answer Scott put down the pumpkin and ran into the bedroom. He was back in a minute holding up the orange paper pumpkin that he had traced and cut out.

"That's wonderful," said Mrs. Winter. "If you make some more you can hang them up around the kitchen for your party. You're a good teacher, Sue Ellen. I'll tell Miss Kelly you're running your own school and planning your own party right here! Goodbye now. Have fun." Mrs. Winter went out the back door and the three little children ran around to a front window to watch her drive away.

Sue Ellen just stood still thinking. She couldn't decide what to do first. Should she try on her new blue jacket, or her black cat costume, or should she finish helping the kids make decorations to hang around the kitchen for their Hallowe'en party?

"I'll put some soup on for us," said Mrs. Stokley, "and we can have the cupcakes and ice cream. That was real nice of your teacher and Mrs. Winter."

Sue Ellen was glad to hear her mother say that because sometimes it just made her mother mad to have people give them things.

Scott came back from watching Mrs. Winter drive away. He was thinking about the witch that had come to the back door. "Me was 'cared of that mon'ter," he said, smiling happily from ear to ear. "Me like to be 'cared!"

8

Reading with Polly

How glad Sue Ellen was to be back in her regular seat on the school bus! Mrs. Carboni had finally given her permission to go back to school. It seemed to Sue Ellen that she had been out forever, but actually she'd been out only a week.

Sue Ellen was wearing her glasses, and her new blue ski jacket and hood. In her hand she was clutching the work sheets that she had done at home. Martha had gotten hold of one of them and had scribbled all over it with her crayon, but Sue Ellen had rescued it before it was completely ruined.

The bus had arrived at the Morristown Center School and the high school boys and girls were crowding on. At first glance Polly didn't recognize Sue Ellen in her new blue jacket. But then she looked again and sat down beside her.

"Good!" said Polly. "I was hoping you'd be back today, Sue Ellen. This is my day to go into your room. I love your new jacket. What do you have in your hand, homework?"

Sue Ellen nodded. She was glad Polly called it homework. She wanted to be like the children in the regular classes. They had homework. She was going to ask Miss Kelly to give her homework all the time, not just when she was out sick.

"I remember when I had work sheets like that," said Polly, glancing at the sheets. "That kind was fun. Perhaps Miss Kelly will let me correct your work with you when I come into your room today."

When Sue Ellen arrived at school, Miss Kelly was not in the room. Sue Ellen put her completed work sheets on the teacher's desk. Then she just stood and looked around the room. Sue Ellen sighed contentedly. It was so wonderful to be back again. Tommy Stroud could call school jail, but it wasn't any jail in Miss Kelly's room. There was food to eat, a place to rest, and fun things happening all the time. Everyone had jobs to do and errands to run, not just Betsy Hall. The fish had to be fed, the mice houses cleaned, and the table set for snacks and parties.

Sheri and Ruth were over in the doll corner. Sheri was dressing a doll. She waved to Sue Ellen and smiled. Sue Ellen had never had such good friends as she had in Miss Kelly's room. Ruth came hurrying over in a pair of high-heeled shoes and a big floppy hat.

"Hi, S-S-Sue Ellen," shouted Ruth, grabbing one of

Sue Ellen's hands. "C-come s-see Sh-She," and Ruth
practically dragged Sue Ellen over to one of the mouse
cages. Ruth pointed to a spot in the wood chips that
was alive with tiny, squirming mice.

"Sh-She had babies! Lots of them," exclaimed Ruth.
"Do you see them?"

Sue Ellen nodded. She could see the naked little
mice babies even though they were almost buried in the
wood chips. Jenny and Tod had just arrived. They
came running over and greeted Sue Ellen happily.

"She had babies," said Jenny. "She's a mummy
now."

"We're going to get money for the babies," said Tod
excitedly. "Mrs. Darwin's class came in to see them
and some of them kids is going to ask their mothers if
they can use our mice. Mr. Flannigan's going to help
us boys build cages. We can make lots of money."

Sue Ellen didn't know what Tod was talking about.
But she did know who Mr. Flannigan was. He was a
retired carpenter, another friend of Miss Kelly's class.
He had begun coming in to help the children with
woodworking projects.

"And look over here," said Jenny, pulling Sue Ellen
by the arm, "the guppy fish had babies too. Miss Kelly
says guppy babies don't want to be with their mummies.
I like to be with my mummy." Jenny was pointing to
a second fish tank that was on the shelf beside the old

one. At first Sue Ellen thought it was empty, but when
she looked more carefully she saw lots of tiny specks
darting about. Tod explained that those were the
guppy babies.

"When they get bigger we'll sell the baby fish," explained Tod. "We're going to make a lot of money
and do things with it."

Miss Kelly had come back into her room now. She
saw Sue Ellen and hurried over to say hello. "My but
it's nice to see you back!" She gave Sue Ellen a big
hug. "A lot happened while you were out. I guess
you've already heard: mice babies, fish babies, and
plans for all of us to become millionaires. We'll tell
you more about it when we're having our snack. Run
along and wash up now."

At snack time Miss Kelly told Sue Ellen about some
of the plans the class had made while she was out of
school. One plan was to have a pet mouse rental serv-
ice. The class was going to rent the baby mice, when
they were big enough, to children in the other classes.
It would cost twenty-five cents a week for a mouse and
a cage. Mr. Flannigan was coming in to help the children make a half-dozen little cages in which to house
the mice. The class was also going to sell guppies for
fifteen cents apiece. Miss Kelly had discovered that
many children in the Parkville School had tropical fish
at home.

Mr. Cohen, the school principal, had announced the class plans over the school intercom so that all of the children in the school knew about them. The boys and girls in Miss Kelly's class were going to keep a record

of the money they made. They were going to put it in
the bank with their other money and at the end of the
year they planned to do some special things with all
the money they had in the bank.

Miss Kelly looked at the big clock on the wall. "The
little hand is on the nine and the big hand is on the
twelve. Who can tell me what time it is?"

Sue Ellen knew she couldn't.

Ruth raised her hand. "N-Nine o'clock," said Ruth.

"Good," said Miss Kelly. "Remember, when the big
hand is on the twelve it is exactly on the hour. The
little hand tells us which hour."

It did not tell Sue Ellen that. If the big hand was
on the twelve, why wasn't it twelve o'clock? Why were
there two hands, anyway? And what did the big hand
have to do with the little hand? Well, at least Sue
Ellen knew all her numbers now and Miss Kelly said
that was a big step forward.

"I want the older children to go over to their desks,"
explained Miss Kelly, "and get out their math papers.
I'll be working with them this morning. We'll figure
out how many guppies we'll have to sell to make a
hundred dollars. Miss Foster, I'd like you to take the
younger group for reading."

As Miss Kelly finished speaking the door of the classroom opened and Polly Smith came in. She went over
and spoke to Miss Kelly. The teacher nodded her

head, picked up Sue Ellen's work sheets from the top of her desk, and handed them to Polly. She also gave her a red marking pencil. Then Miss Kelly went over to explain to Miss Foster that Polly was going to be working with Sue Ellen for a little while this morning.

Sue Ellen was glad. Polly was like an extra big sister, only she was lots nicer to her than her own sister, Victoria. The two girls carried a desk and two chairs over into the doll corner so they could have a quiet place to work. Polly put the work sheets on the desk and she and Sue Ellen began to go over them together.

The first paper that Sue Ellen had done had six large letters down the side. The letters were: H, M, F, B, C, S. Across from each letter there was a row of four pictures. Sue Ellen was supposed to draw a line from the letter to the picture that began with that letter.

"First," suggested Polly, "why don't you tell me the name and then the sound of each of the letters? If you have those right the rest is easy."

Sue Ellen looked at the page. She had practiced the sounds many times at home. One day, when Ma wasn't feeling so bad, she had listened to Sue Ellen sound out the letters. Ma knew how to read. Sue Ellen felt quite sure of herself. "The H says h-h-h; the M says m-m-m; the F says f-f-f; the B says b-b-b; the C says c-c-c; and the S says s-s-s."

"Perfect!" said Polly, clapping her hands. Miss

Kelly had explained to Polly that it was important to praise the children in her class when they did something well. She said that most of these children were so used to failing and not being able to keep up with other children that they had lost all confidence in themselves.

"Even after a week out of school you knew them all! That's fine, Sue Ellen," continued Polly. "Now, let's check and see whether or not you have drawn the line from the letter to the picture that begins with that letter."

Beside the H there was a picture of a cow, a house, a dog, and a barn. Sue Ellen had drawn her line from the H to the house. It was a pretty little white house with an upstairs and a downstairs, and a screened porch.

"The first one is right," said Polly. " 'House' begins with the h-h-h sound. You may put a correct mark at the end of the first row." Polly gave Sue Ellen the red marker.

Sue Ellen knew exactly how Miss Foster made a correct mark and she made hers look just like Miss Foster's.

The second letter was an M. Beside it were pictures of a lamb, a pig, a truck, and a pretty young woman holding a baby. Sue Ellen's line went from the M to the woman with the baby.

Polly thought she would see if Sue Ellen could explain why she had drawn the line to the woman. She asked, "Why did you have your line go there?"

Sue Ellen was worried. Had she made a mistake? "Ain't her the baby's ma? Ma starts with m-m-m sound, don't it?"

"You're right," said Polly with a smile. "You could have thought it was a lady, 'lady' begins with L; or a woman, and 'woman' begins with W. But because she had a baby in her arms, you must have figured out she was a mother. That was good thinking, Sue Ellen. You may put a correct mark at the end of that row, too."

The next letter was F and the pictures beside it showed a boat, an airplane, a cat, and a man with a hat on carrying a little bag and waving good-bye to some children. Sue Ellen had drawn her line from the F to the man.

"Why did you draw the line to the man?" asked Polly. "Doesn't 'man' start with M?"

This time Sue Ellen wasn't worried. She wasn't going to let Polly's questions scare her. "Because him's the father and 'father' begins with f-f-f."

"Good for you," said Polly. "He *is* the father. You have them all right so far." Polly thought Sue Ellen had done very well to figure out the pictures on the work sheets. Polly knew Sue Ellen's house certainly did not look like the neat little white house on the work sheet, and her mother was not young and pretty. Polly knew that Sue Ellen's father never carried a briefcase or waved good-bye to his family when he left for work. He wore overalls and he left for work when it was still dark and his family was still fast asleep.

Sue Ellen had finished making another large correct mark at the end of the third row. She had none wrong so far. "Now we have a B," said Polly. "Let's see what you did with this one."

Beside the B there was a picture of a window, a four-poster bed with a canopy over the top, a trunk, and a pair of socks. Sue Ellen had drawn her line from the B to the trunk. Polly was about to put a big X mark at the end of this line when she stopped herself. Perhaps Sue Ellen had a reason for doing what she had done. "Why did you draw the line to that picture?" Polly asked.

"Because box begins with B," said Sue Ellen confidently.

"Oh," said Polly. "I see. You know, Sue Ellen, when I did work sheets like these, sometimes I couldn't figure out what the picture was supposed to show. And sometimes our family didn't call the things by the same name as the person who made up the work sheets. I remember one in which the letter was S and there was a picture of a couch. At least that's what we called it in our family. But you were supposed to call it a sofa. So I got it wrong and even when I explained why to the teacher, she still called it wrong. I didn't think that was fair."

Sue Ellen nodded her head. She knew what Polly was talking about. Lots of times her papers were marked wrong because she had never seen the things in the pictures, or she didn't know the names that other people knew for them.

"That is supposed to be a picture of a trunk, not a box," explained Polly. "Like the trunk over there that Miss Kelly has the dress-up clothes in, see?"

Sue Ellen had never before realized that that was called a trunk. They didn't have trunks at her house. She said the word out loud. "Trunk. 'Trunk' begins with a T not a B."

"That's right," said Polly. She began to erase the line that Sue Ellen had drawn from the B to the trunk.

"Oh, no!" protested Sue Ellen. "You ain't supposed to erase the wrong ones. Miss Foster puts a big X on them."

"That's all right," said Polly, continuing with her erasing. "If you didn't know that was a trunk and thought it was a box you didn't have it wrong; you had it right. 'Box' does begin with B."

But Sue Ellen looked worried. She still didn't think that Polly should erase that line. How could it be right and wrong at the same time?

"I'll explain about it to Miss Foster afterwards," said Polly, noticing Sue Ellen's worried expression. Polly finished erasing the line. "Now, look at the four pictures again and find the one that begins with a B."

Sue Ellen looked at the window, and — well, she didn't know what that second thing was — then the trunk, and finally the pair of socks. Probably it was the second thing that began with the B, but she really didn't know what it was. Perhaps it was a little house. It had a kind of roof. But house begins with the h-h-h sound. Sue Ellen couldn't decide what to do. If she just guessed, Polly might ask her *why* she had drawn the line where she did and she wouldn't have any reason. When she was in Mrs. Perry's class all she ever did was guess the answers and she almost always guessed them wrong.

Polly could see that Sue Ellen was having trouble. "Why don't you say the name of each of the pictures out loud?"

Sue Ellen began. "Window. That ain't it; window starts with W." She paused. "I don't know what that next thing is, Polly."

Polly was surprised that Sue Ellen didn't recognize the bed with the canopy top. One of Polly's friends had a four-poster canopy bed just like it. "That's a bed, Sue Ellen. It's a kind some people had in the olden days before houses had furnaces. They put a roof and curtains all around their beds to help them keep warm. It made it like a little room. Some people have them nowadays just to be fancy, but they don't usually put curtains around them any more."

"Oh," said Sue Ellen. "That's supposed to be a bed?" Her face brightened up as she said the word out loud. "Bed. 'Bed' begins with B."

"Right," said Polly, handing Sue Ellen a pencil. "Go ahead now and draw the line where it should be. I don't know why they didn't draw a sensible looking bed in the first place. And you may put a correct mark at the end of that line, too."

Sue Ellen drew the line from the B to the bed. She really didn't think she should give herself a correct mark, but she did want to get a 100 if she could, so she did as Polly said.

The next letter was S. Sue Ellen had drawn her line to the first picture, which was a shiny white stove. While Sue Ellen put the red check at the end of that line Polly was thinking of something that Mrs. Winter had told her mother. Mrs. Winter had been terribly upset the day she had gone to the Stokleys' with Sue Ellen's Hallowe'en things to find that Mrs. Stokley was cooking on a hot plate. This meant that there was no oven and Mrs. Stokley couldn't cook cheap, nourishing things like baked potatoes or casseroles. Mostly she or Henry just fried or boiled things. There was a chance that Polly's mother could get an electric stove free in a few months. A woman over in Parkville was redoing her kitchen and had offered to give her old stove to the high school. The stove was perfectly good but they didn't need another one at the high school. Polly hoped that Sue Ellen's family could have the stove instead.

"There's one more letter," said Sue Ellen, reminding Polly of what she was supposed to be doing. It was the letter C. Beside it were pictures of a dog, a car, a train, and a speedboat. Sue Ellen had correctly drawn her line to the car.

Polly took the red marking crayon and made a correct mark at the end of the line. Then she wrote a great big "100%" across the top of the paper. "That's wonderful!" said Polly. "You should be very proud of yourself, Sue Ellen. You really are almost ready to read."

At just that minute the fire alarm bell rang. Sue Ellen looked terrified. She was afraid of fires. Scott liked to play with matches and he had set fire to the Stokleys' house twice already. Both times Henry had discovered it in time and put the fire out.

Polly took Sue Ellen's hand. "Come on, it's probably just a fire drill," she whispered. Polly was right. As they stood shivering in the school yard, Mr. Cohen congratulated them all on their speedy and orderly exit. When the fire drill was over, it was recess time. Sue

Ellen waved good-bye to Polly and hurried back to her classroom for her new blue jacket. If she hurried, she might get a swing.

9

Laying Plans

SUE ELLEN was watching the big flat snowflakes drift lazily down outside the classroom window. They were coming down so slowly that Sue Ellen thought perhaps it was going to stop snowing. She hoped so. She was tired of snow.

Miss Kelly had told the class that today, February 2nd, was a special day. She had put a picture of a fat woodchuck up on the bulletin board. Miss Kelly called it a groundhog, and she said that today was Groundhog Day. Sue Ellen remembered the woodchuck that had run across the road in front of Martha and her one day. That was the closest she had ever come to one. But there were lots of woodchucks near her house, and the field across the road was full of woodchuck holes.

Usually the sun shone in the two big windows in Miss Kelly's room. Sometimes on sunny days the class played with their shadows on the floor in front of the windows. They stepped on each other's shadows and played shadow tag. But this morning, when Miss Kelly asked Sue Ellen to stand in front of the windows, she didn't have any shadow.

Miss Kelly asked the children if they thought Mr. Groundhog had been able to see his shadow this morning when he came up out of his hole where he had been sleeping all winter long. They decided that he couldn't see his shadow without the sun. Miss Kelly explained that people used to think that if the groundhog sees his shadow when he comes up out of his hole on February 2nd, his own shadow frightens him and he runs back into his hole and winter lasts for six more weeks; but if he doesn't see his shadow, he stays out of his hole, and there is no more winter.

While Sue Ellen was daydreaming about woodchucks and spring, Doreen was reading out loud to the class. It wasn't easy for Sue Ellen to listen to someone read. Before she started going to school no one had ever read her a story. When she was in Mrs. Perry's room even noisy Tommy Stroud would sit quietly and listen when Mrs. Perry read a story. But not Sue Ellen! She would sort things in her desk, or slip out of her chair onto the floor, or put her head down on her desk and go to sleep.

At the beginning of the year in Miss Kelly's class almost no one except Patrick and some of the older children would even stay at their desks for more than

a few minutes. Miss Kelly couldn't possibly have read stories to them.

But already it was different! A little while after Hallowe'en, in the morning when they all sat around the tables having their snack, Miss Kelly had begun telling them short stories about when she was a little girl. At first she told the same stories over and over. Sue Ellen liked the one about the time Miss Kelly got lost in the woods; and the one about the time her cat had kittens in her bed; and the one about the time she broke her arm playing train on some chairs with her brother.

Usually, now, even Tod and Jenny would sit still and listen to stories. And sometimes Miss Kelly asked them to tell her stories, not great long ones, but short ones about themselves. At first Sue Ellen hadn't wanted to tell a story, but finally she'd been brave enough to tell about the day she had seen the snapping turtle in the pond.

Today Miss Kelly had asked Doreen to read to the whole class. She was reading part of a booklet about a farm. It was not as easy to listen to Doreen read as to Miss Kelly. She didn't make her voice go up and down right. The farm that Doreen was reading about was a special kind of farm, one that children could visit and explore. They could give a baby lamb a bottle of milk, or see baby chickens hatch out of eggs. They might even be able to milk a goat or a cow. It was a real place and it cost money to go there. It was called The Pet Farm, and Miss Kelly's class might take a trip there at the end of the year.

When Doreen finished reading, Miss Kelly said: "Thank you, Doreen. Your reading is improving all the time. What do you think, class? Do you think we should go to The Pet Farm?"

"Yes! Let's go there," exclaimed Jenny, clapping her hands. "That's where I want us to go."

Sue Ellen thought she'd like to go there, too.

"It is a wonderful place," agreed Miss Kelly. "I've been there and I know you children would love it. But we must find out whether or not we have enough money to go. We may need to earn extra money for the trip."

"We can use the money in the bank," said Tod, jumping up. "We have a lot of money in the bank."

"We *had* a lot of money in the bank," corrected Miss Kelly. "But don't forget; I bought our wood supply, our tropical fish, and our mice with some of our money. We've bought bread, and jam and peanut butter for our snacks, and we've bought fresh supplies for our grocery store several times. We had our Hallowe'en lunch party and our Christmas party, and we have had birthday parties for eight of our class so far. We hired a school bus to take us to the airport once and we'll have to hire a bus to take us to The Pet Farm. We'll also have to pay to get in. I imagine the trip to the farm will cost us at least thirty-five dollars."

"How much money do we have left in the bank now?" asked Miss Foster.

"Let me see," said Miss Kelly. She took the class bank book out of her top desk drawer and studied it for a minute. "We have $38.20. That includes the $12.50 we've made on our mice and guppies so far."

That seemed like a lot of money to Sue Ellen. Surely it was enough for their trip.

"Is that enough money for us to go?" asked Jenny, impatiently. "I hope it's enough."

"We need more than just enough money to go on the trip," cautioned Miss Foster. "Don't forget, we'll want to have a Valentine party and an Easter party, and there are several people who haven't had birthday parties yet." Sue Ellen was one of them. She didn't want to miss out on her birthday party.

"That's right," agreed Miss Kelly. "I think we are definitely going to need more money." She looked around at the disappointed faces of her class. Jenny looked ready to cry. "Cheer up, all of you. I have an idea of how we might earn the extra money we need. The other day after school Miss Foster, Mrs. Winter, Mrs. Briggs, Mr. Flannigan, and I had a meeting about this very problem. We wondered how you would like to give an auction to raise money."

"Yes, yes!" shouted several of the older children. "Let's have an auction."

Patrick raised his hand.

"Yes, Patrick," said Miss Kelly.

"What's an auction?" Patrick had moved to Parkville from the city after his father left home. He had never been to a country auction.

Sue Ellen had been to one with Pa and the kids last summer. She hadn't really understood what was going on. She just knew it was exciting. A big fat man sat up front surrounded by tables and chairs and dishes and things. He talked very fast and everybody shouted numbers at him. Pa had gotten the hot plate for Ma and a better crib for Martha at that auction.

"Auctioning is a way of selling things," explained Miss Kelly. "Auctions are fun. Come on, Miss Foster, let's you and I and Doreen show Patrick and the rest of the class how an auction works." Miss Kelly walked over and whispered to Doreen for a minute. Then the teacher looked around for something to sell. She picked up her own desk chair and held it up in the air.

"All set now. I'm the auctioneer and Miss Foster and Doreen are the people at the auction. Here's a lovely oak chair. Who will give me a dollar for this fine chair? Let's start the bidding at a dollar. Who will give me a dollar?"

"Fifty cents!" shouted Doreen.

"All right, fifty cents. I have fifty cents," said Miss Kelly. "Who will give me a dollar?"

"A dollar," Miss Foster called out.

"A dollar-fifty," shouted Doreen.

Miss Foster didn't say anything. Sue Ellen hoped Miss Foster was going to get the chair.

"I have a dollar-fifty," repeated Miss Kelly. "Who will give me two dollars? This chair would cost you a lot more than two dollars in a store. Who will give me two dollars, two dollars?"

Suddenly Jenny jumped up and shouted. "Five dollars. I'll give you five dollars. I'll ask my mummy for five dollars."

"You only need to bid two dollars, Jenny," explained Miss Kelly, smiling. "All right, I have two dollars from this fine young lady here in the front row." Miss Kelly waited a minute for a higher bid, and then she added, "Going, going, gone! For two dollars to Miss Jenny Briggs." Miss Kelly handed the chair to Jenny. "Thank you, Jenny, for playing our auction game with us. Perhaps you'll make bids when we have our real auction." Turning to Patrick she asked, "Do you see how an auction works now, Patrick? The auctioneer sells the things to whoever will bid the most money for them."

Sue Ellen was sure an auction would be fun.

Patrick had his hand raised again. "We couldn't

really sell your chair at our auction, could we? Where
would we get things to sell?"

"No, of course we couldn't. You're right. We certainly would need things to sell. At our meeting we
came up with several ideas. For example, Mr. Flannigan suggested that you children could easily make more
wooden boot jacks, bird feeders, and bird houses. He
said that he'd be glad to be in charge of that project.
Mrs. Briggs agreed to work with a group making
baked goods. She thought cakes, pies, and cookies would
sell well. Mrs. Winter and I have a lot of friends in
town who would give us old furniture and dishes and
things like that. We might have to fix up some of the
furniture before we sold it, but that would give us good
experience. Perhaps you children will think of other
things we could sell."

Sue Ellen couldn't think of anything but Sheri raised
her hand.

"Yes, Sheri," said Miss Kelly.

"I'd like to make more potholders to sell."

"That's a good idea," agreed Miss Kelly. "Your potholders are so pretty. I'm sure we could sell a lot of
them. I thought of something else, too. Don't you
think it would be nice if we asked Father Tom to practice four or five of our favorite folk songs with us regu-
larly? Then we could give a short musical program the
night of the auction."

This idea was greeted enthusiastically. Sue Ellen was especially excited at the idea of having the auction at night in the big auditorium. Children from the other classes, parents, brothers and sisters, and friends from all the towns around would be invited. The pupils in Miss Kelly's class had been invited to programs put on by other classes, but they had never been the ones to put on the program. Sue Ellen had always wanted to be one of the important people up on the stage.

Sue Ellen had her hand raised now. She was surprised at how often she raised her hand in Miss Kelly's class. She had never raised her hand in Mrs. Perry's room because she had never felt that she was part of what was going on.

"Yes, Sue Ellen?" said Miss Kelly.

"Will the auction be next week?"

"Oh, dear, no!" exclaimed Miss Kelly. Although Sue Ellen was beginning to use words like yesterday and tomorrow, and was beginning to know the days of the week, she still had very little real sense of time. "The auction can't possibly be for weeks and weeks, or maybe even months and months. It will be in the spring sometime. It's going to take a lot of work to get ready for it."

"I'm all ready now," said Jenny. "I want to have the auction soon."

"I have an idea," said Miss Kelly. "Let's make a list together on the blackboard of some of the things we'll have to do to get ready for the auction. Perhaps that will help Jenny and Sue Ellen understand how much work and how much time something like this takes. Miss Foster, will you write down the things as the children suggest them? Raise your hand when you've thought of something we'll have to do before we can have the auction."

By the time Miss Foster had reached the bottom of the blackboard the list looked like this:

INVITE PEOPLE TO COME.
DECIDE WHERE AND WHEN THE AUCTION WILL BE.
COOK THINGS.
MAKE MORE POTHOLDERS.
MAKE THINGS OUT OF WOOD. PAINT THEM. BUY
    MORE PAINT.
PRACTICE OUR SONGS WITH FATHER TOM.
MAKE SIGNS FOR THE AUCTION AND HANG THEM
    UP AROUND TOWN.
ASK MR. COHEN TO ANNOUNCE THE AUCTION ON
    HIS INTERCOM.
GET LOTS OF OTHER THINGS TO SELL.

"Probably there are more things that we haven't even thought of," said Miss Kelly, "but these ought to be enough to show us why we couldn't possibly have the auction next week."

Sue Ellen was disappointed. She didn't like things that took a long time. Nobody in her family did.

Miss Foster had another idea. "I think we should think about our list a little more and write it over again with the things we'll need to do first at the beginning of the list and the things we'll want to do last near the end of the list."

Miss Kelly agreed that this would be a good idea. When they were finished with their thinking, the new list looked like this:

MAKE THINGS OUT OF WOOD. BUY PAINT. PAINT THEM.

MAKE MORE POTHOLDERS.

COLLECT OTHER THINGS TO SELL. REPAIR AND PAINT THEM.

PRACTICE OUR SONGS WITH FATHER TOM.

DECIDE WHERE AND WHEN THE AUCTION WILL BE.

ASK MR. COHEN TO ANNOUNCE IT.

MAKE SIGNS FOR THE AUCTION AND POST THEM.

INVITE PEOPLE TO COME.

COOK THINGS.

Everyone in the class agreed that cooking was one of the last things they would need to do.

Tod raised his hand.

"Yes?" said Miss Kelly.

"When it's time, can I make a cake for the auction?"

Two of the big boys began to laugh. "What are you two boys laughing at?" asked Miss Kelly, a little impatiently.

"Boys don't cook," said David.

"Of course they cook!" said Miss Kelly. "Some of the most famous cooks in the world have been men. My father was a much better cook than my mother was."

Sue Ellen knew that was true. Her father could cook better than her mother when he wanted to, and Henry was a better cook than Victoria.

"You know," continued Miss Kelly, "some of you older children will be going into high school next year. When you're over there you have to begin to think about the kinds of jobs you'd like when you finish school. There are jobs waiting for good cooks. Who knows, someday we may all go out to dinner at 'Tod's Tip Top Restaurant'!"

Sue Ellen had her hand up again.

"Yes, Sue Ellen?"

"Can I make a cake, too?"

"Of course you may. You might even be able to read the directions yourself when the time comes."

Sue Ellen was looking out the window. Even though

the woodchuck hadn't seen his shadow it was still snowing. All that snow would have to melt before it was
spring and before it was time for the auction.

10

Crazy Cake

THE SNOW did finally melt, but not until April. And even then Miss Kelly's class was not ready for the auction. For another month they sawed and hammered and sanded and painted. They washed dishes and vases that had been tucked away in people's attics and cellars for years and years.

Sometimes they hammered their fingers instead of the nails and painted their noses instead of the chairs. Sometimes they broke dishes and cracked vases, but Miss Kelly said accidents were bound to happen when anyone took on a job as big as this one.

Some of the getting ready was fun, but a lot of it was just plain hard work. There were days when Sue Ellen never wanted to hear the word auction again, and there were days when even sandpapering and dish-drying were fun. Gradually what had once seemed like a great big classroom began to look like an over-crowded store. And by the beginning of May, Miss

Kelly was finally ready to name the exact date for the auction. She chose the twenty-fifth of May.

Then out went invitations in the mail; up went signs around the whole town; and over the air went announcements on Mr. Cohen's intercom — COME TO THE SPECIAL CLASS AUCTION. MAY 25TH AT 7:30 P.M. IN THE PARKVILLE ELEMENTARY SCHOOL AUDITORIUM.

On the morning of May twenty-fifth, at nine o'clock, Sue Ellen and Polly were standing in front of the kitchen table in Miss Kelly's room. Sue Ellen knew it was nine o'clock because the big hand was on the twelve and the little hand was on the nine. Sue Ellen understood about the big hand now — just as long as it was right on the twelve. But if the big hand was on the eleven, or on the one, or any number other than the twelve, then Sue Ellen got all mixed up with the "of's" and the "after's."

Sue Ellen was all ready to make the cake that she was going to sell at the auction tonight. She was wearing her pretty pink checkered cooking apron. Over at the other big table Tod was getting ready to make his cake with Mrs. Briggs. He had on an apron too, a boy's white cooking apron. On the front in large letters was printed "COME AND GET IT." Sue Ellen could read all of those words. Soon after Groundhog Day Polly's mother had invited the older girls from Miss

Kelly's class into her Home Ec room to make aprons with some of her girls. Everyone in Miss Kelly's class had wanted an apron made, even the big boys.

Sue Ellen had a piece of cardboard propped up in front of her. On it, in large clear letters, Polly had printed the recipe for the cake and frosting that Sue Ellen was going to make. She could read a few of the words herself — cup, salt, oil — but most of the words were still too difficult. Polly would have to read the directions to her.

"Let's get started, Sue Ellen," said Polly. "First of all, we set our oven at 350°, that's three-five-zero."

Sue Ellen turned the dial to the correct temperature. She felt very important setting the oven temperature herself. She had used the electric stove several times now. She had made baked potatoes twice and she had made a muffin mix and a gingerbread mix. Miss Kelly wanted Sue Ellen to do more and more things by herself on the stove because the Stokleys were soon going to have an electric stove of their own. If her mother would let her, Sue Ellen might be able to make a few simple things on the stove at home.

"You need a 350° oven, too, don't you, Mrs. Briggs?" Polly called over to the two workers at the other table.

"Yes, we do," answered Mrs. Briggs. "Our cake cooks at the same temperature as yours, and for the same length of time, too, forty minutes."

"Good," said Polly. "Let's try to get them into the oven together. Now, Sue Ellen, I think we have everything we need on the table in front of us. You set out a measuring cup, measuring spoons, a fork, and a square pan. I put out the flour, cocoa, sugar, soda, salt, oil, vinegar, vanilla, and a cup of cold water." As Polly named the ingredients, she touched each one. She wanted Sue Ellen to learn the names of the things she was pointing at. But Sue Ellen was so excited — everyone in Miss Kelly's room was excited today — that she really wasn't listening to Polly at all.

"I'll read the directions to you and help with the measuring," Polly continued, "but if it is to be your cake, you must do as much as you can yourself. It's really an easy cake to make. I've been making it ever since I was as old as you are. It's called 'Crazy Cake,' " and Polly pointed to the two words printed in large letters at the top of the cardboard.

"Crazy Cake," said Sue Ellen. Suddenly she was paying attention. "Crazy Cake," she repeated again slowly. She was quiet for a minute. Then she looked up at Polly. There was something she wanted to know. She would ask Polly. "Victoria says that everybody in this class is crazy. She calls us 'crazy retards.' Are we?"

Sue Ellen's question took Polly by surprise. For a minute all she could say was, "Oh." Lots of times Polly

had heard boys and girls from the other classes call the
children in Miss Kelly's class "crazy" or "nummies" or
"tards." More than once she had scolded Andy Stroud,
Tommy's big brother, for doing it. Polly had never
even thought of the name of the cake when she'd chosen
it. What should she say now?

Sue Ellen was waiting for Polly's answer. Sue Ellen
loved Miss Kelly, and she loved being in the special
class. She had never had such good friends as she had
this year at school. What would Polly say?

Polly began to speak. "Lots of people use the word
'crazy' when they just mean 'different.' Some of my
friends think I'm crazy because my ideas are different
from theirs. And just the other day I heard one of the
teachers say that Miss Kelly certainly had some crazy
ideas about teaching."

"Miss Kelly is the best teacher in the whole world!"
said Sue Ellen. She wasn't going to let anyone say anything mean about Miss Kelly.

"Of course she is," agreed Polly. "You and I know
that. The other teachers just meant that Miss Kelly's
ideas about teaching were different from most teachers'.
And they are. Her room is different from any other
room in school and loads more fun. You learn more in
it, too. You're beginning to read. Mrs. Perry couldn't
teach you to read. And Sheri was so shy she was afraid
of her own shadow, but now she isn't. Sure the kids in

here are a little different. They have bigger problems. And this cake is a little different from other cakes. That's why it is called 'Crazy Cake.' "

"Hey! You two had better stop talking and get cooking," Tod called over from the other table. "We're way ahead of you." Tod had flour all over his face. He was sifting more flour into a larger bowl.

"You've got flour on the end of your nose," Sue Ellen called out. Then she added, "You look crazy!"

Polly laughed. "He does look different! But Tod's right. Even though our cake is quicker than his, we'd better hurry," and Polly began to read off the directions.

Sue Ellen tried hard to concentrate. With Polly's help she measured the flour, cocoa, soda, sugar, and salt into the sifter. Then she turned the little handle and sifted the dry mixture directly into the cake pan.

"That's the first crazy thing about this cake," explained Polly, " — sifting right into the pan in which you are going to cook it. Usually the flour is sifted into a bowl first, but by doing it this way there isn't any dirty bowl to wash. The next step is crazy, too. The directions say to 'make three holes in the dry mixture.' Make a big one, a middle-sized one, and a little one, just like in Goldilocks and the three bears. Use the back of the big measuring spoon to make the holes."

Sue Ellen knew the story of Goldilocks and the three

bears. Miss Kelly had read it to the class one day. She made the three holes very carefully. Then, while she held the measuring spoons, Polly poured in, first the oil, then the vinegar, and finally the vanilla. Sue Ellen emptied each of the liquids into the three holes.

"They look like three little ponds," said Sue Ellen, admiring her handiwork.

"Only now we're going to flood the ponds," said Polly. "The directions say to 'pour the cold water over it all, and beat with a fork until it is smooth and the white flour doesn't show.' "

Sue Ellen poured the water over the whole mixture. "Now it looks like one of Scott's mud pies," said Sue Ellen, as she began to stir it all together with the fork.

"Let's hope it isn't going to taste like one, though," laughed Polly. "Here, let me get you started. It's difficult not to stir too hard and have the batter spill over the sides of the pan. I'll get the flour out of the corners and then you can finish it off. My mother used to have to help me on this part."

After Polly had mixed the cake batter carefully, Sue Ellen gave it a few more stirs. Polly opened the oven door and Sue Ellen put her cake in. "We beat you, Tod," said Sue Ellen as she closed the oven door.

"Not by much," said Mrs. Briggs. "Open up the oven door again. Here comes Tod's cake. Set the timer for forty minutes, someone." Polly turned the timer on

CRAZY CAKE

1½ cups flour   6 tablespoons oil
3 tablespoons cocoa   1 tablespoon vinegar
1 teaspoon soda   1 teaspoon vanilla
1 cup sugar   1 cup cold water
      ½ teaspoon salt

Sift flour, cocoa, soda, sugar, salt into ungreased 9x9x2 inch cake pan. Make three holes in the dry mixture. Into one, pour the oil, into another, pour the vinegar, into the third, pour the vanilla.

Pour the cold water over it all and beat until smooth and no white flour shows. Bake for 40 minutes at 350°.

PLAIN BUTTER FROSTING

¼ cup butter or oleo
2 cups confectioner's sugar
3 tablespoons milk
¼ teaspoon vanilla

Work butter or oleo with fork until soft. Add a cup of sugar and a tablespoon of milk and stir. Continue until all sugar and milk are gone. Add vanilla and spread on cake.

the stove so it would sound when the cakes were done.

"Sue Ellen," said Mrs. Briggs, "if you'll take your few dirty dishes over to the sink, Tod will wash them with his. You can do the drying for him." Mrs. Briggs was busy wiping off the table where she and Tod had been working. She was getting ready for her next cooks, Ruth and Sheri. They were going to cut out some cookie dough that had been chilling in the refrigerator.

Sue Ellen loved all the busyness and excitement in the room today. Miss Kelly, with Jenny at her heels, was hurrying back and forth between the classroom and the auditorium. In the auditorium the big boys and Mr. Nelson, the janitor, were setting up chairs and tables. All the furniture and household goods for the auction had been taken up onto the stage. Miss Foster and the older girls were arranging the things as attractively as possible. Sue Ellen would rather have been running back and forth with Miss Kelly and Jenny than drying dishes with Tod, but she didn't quite dare slip away.

When Sue Ellen and Tod had finished washing dishes, Polly asked Sue Ellen to come over to the ironing board. Polly was shaking out a white party dress. "This is the dress you picked out to wear tonight," said Polly. "It's clean but it needs to be ironed. Miss Kelly asked me to help you iron it. We'll put it on a hanger and take it home with us after school."

Polly and her mother had invited Sue Ellen to have supper at their house. Then Sue Ellen would dress for the auction and come back with them. Mr. and Mrs. Stokley had said they would try to come to the auction, but Miss Kelly didn't want to take the chance that Sue Ellen might miss the auction. Sue Ellen didn't know it, but Polly's mother had a surprise waiting for her: a pair of brand-new black patent leather shoes, and new white socks to wear with her party dress tonight.

Polly showed Sue Ellen how hot to have her iron, how to hold it so she wouldn't burn herself, and how to do a neat job. It was not easy for Sue Ellen because she was so short and the iron was so big in her hand, and, to make matters worse, she was left-handed. They had an iron at Sue Ellen's house but Victoria was the only one who ever used it. Sue Ellen was just finishing her ironing when the timer went off.

"Our cakes are done," shouted Tod, jumping up from his desk where he was making a sign. Sue Ellen dropped her iron and rushed after Tod. She didn't want her cake to burn up.

"Come right straight back here, young lady," called Polly, standing the iron up before it had a chance to scorch the dress. "You can't run off and leave a hot iron like that. Finish your dress, shut off your iron, and put your dress on a hanger. Tod and Mrs. Briggs will get the cakes out of the oven."

Sometimes Sue Ellen thought Polly was almost as bossy as Victoria, but she did come back and do as Polly asked.

A few minutes later as Sue Ellen and Tod stood admiring their freshly-baked cakes, the bell for recess sounded. Neither one of them wanted to go out and play. They were sure they were needed inside helping. But Mrs. Briggs said that they could help most by going outside to play. Their cakes could cool in the pans until they came in. Then they could take them out and frost them.

Sue Ellen's cake came out of the pan beautifully. Tod's stuck in one place, but Mrs. Briggs said it wasn't a bit serious and they could patch it up perfectly with frosting. Polly had gone back to her own class, so Mrs. Briggs helped both Sue Ellen and Tod with their frostings. They made the plain butter frosting that was printed on Sue Ellen's recipe sheet. Sue Ellen scattered chocolate jimmies over the top of her cake, and Tod cut up red cherries and arranged them on the top of his. Mrs. Briggs said that at her house when she and Jenny cooked, Jenny always got some "pay" at the end. The pay today was a whole cherry for each of

them, a handful of jimmies, and of course the frosting
bowls to clean out. Sue Ellen had a slight stomach
ache when she was finished.

At two o'clock in the afternoon, Miss Kelly's class
walked into the auditorium for their final rehearsal.
Father Tom was there so they could practice their
songs one last time. Mrs. Winter was sitting back at
the far end of the hall. Her job was to make sure that
everyone could be heard.

Miss Kelly had decided to have the curtains closed
across the front of the stage until all the people arrived.
Then she wanted the curtains to open on a scene in
which the children in the class would all be pretending
to be at work getting ready for the auction. In this
way, explained Miss Kelly, the people would have
some idea of how much work had gone into the prepa-
rations for the auction.

When Miss Kelly and Miss Foster had everyone
placed on the stage just the way they wanted them, Miss
Kelly called back to Mrs. Winter, "How do they look?"

"Wonderful!" said Mrs. Winter.

"Fine," said Miss Kelly. "Now let's pretend that
every chair in the hall is filled and we'll go through
our program as if this were the real thing." Miss
Kelly looked at her watch. "And in just about five
hours it will be!"

A shiver of excitement ran down Sue Ellen's back.

11

The Auction

THE CURTAINS were closed. Everyone in Miss Kelly's class was finding his place on the stage. Sue Ellen was already in hers. She was spinning around on the toes of her shiny new shoes watching the skirt of her party dress balloon out around her. Even the bottoms of her shoes were shiny. Sue Ellen could not remember ever having had a pair of brand-new shoes before. She stopped spinning. She was mussing up her hair. Polly had curled it and fixed it with a white ribbon to match her white party dress and new white socks. Sue Ellen felt like a queen.

Suddenly Jenny ran up to the curtains and put her head through the slit in the center. She looked out into the noisy auditorium, and then, just as suddenly, pulled her head back in and ran over to Miss Kelly. "It's full, Miss Kelly. It's full! The whole room is full! I'm so exciting. I feel sick."

"You're not sick, Jenny," laughed Miss Kelly. "And

you're not exciting, just *excited*. So am I. Now be a good girl and stay away from those curtains."

"I'm scared, too," said Sue Ellen running over to Jenny. "Did you see my father and mother out there, Jenny? They said they was coming. Can I look, Miss Kelly?"

"I'll look for you," offered Tod, running over from his place behind Sue Ellen.

"Oh no you won't," said Miss Kelly firmly, catching Tod by the arm. "Every one of you get right back in your places. We're ready to begin. Father Tom, are you ready?"

"Yes, I'm ready," said Father Tom, smiling. He played one or two chords on his guitar to make sure it was in tune. He didn't seem excited or scared. He seemed very calm and relaxed as he always did. It made Sue Ellen feel better just to look at him.

Miss Kelly walked over and stood at the side of the stage. She signaled to Doreen to begin the evening's program. Sue Ellen watched Doreen walk to the center of the stage, feel for the opening in the heavy curtains, and then disappear beyond them.

People in the audience must have noticed Doreen because Sue Ellen heard someone say loudly: "Sh-sh-sh, sh-sh-sh, it's going to begin," and the buzz of conversation on the other side of the curtains died away.

"Good evening, ladies and gentlemen," Doreen be-

gan. Sue Ellen almost knew the speech herself. She
had heard Doreen say it so many times. "Thank you
for coming to our auction tonight." Then Doreen
stopped. Not a sound came from the other side of the
curtains. Sue Ellen's mind went blank, too. Oh dear!
What came next? What if Doreen couldn't remember?
Would the auction be spoiled?

Then Sue Ellen heard Miss Kelly whisper loudly:
"We are selling . . ." Doreen must have heard the
prompting too. She began again. "We are selling
things that we have cooked, things we have made out
of wood, things we have painted and fixed up, and
other things, too."

Doreen took a deep breath and then hurried on.
"With the money that we make, we are going to go on
a trip, buy some things for our room, and if we make a
lot of money, some of us are going to camp this summer." Her speech was almost finished. In a whisper
Sue Ellen repeated the last line with Doreen. "Thank
you for helping us to help ourselves."

That was the end of Doreen's speech. The audience
clapped enthusiastically. Sue Ellen could see Doreen's
fingers fumbling for the slit in the curtains. She found
it and rejoined her class on the stage. Jenny jumped up
to give Doreen a quick hug and then ran back to her
own place.

Sue Ellen's cheeks were burning with excitement.

Her eyes were on Miss Kelly. Now Miss Kelly was signaling to David. He was stationed by the curtain ropes. First he pulled the wrong rope and made the curtain close tighter! Then he found the right rope and the curtains opened!

Thundering applause swept up from the auditorium engulfing the members of Miss Kelly's class like a big wave. Sue Ellen could almost feel it as she stood by her blue painted stool pretending to paint. She was holding a paint brush in her hand, but of course it didn't have any paint on it. As her hand worked automatically back and forth she looked out into the sea of faces in front of her. She couldn't see anything clearly, but she heard her brother, Henry, somewhere near the front of the hall whisper excitedly: "Look, there's Sue Ellen. See her, Ma? Pa, there's Sue Ellen!"

Sue Ellen was happy. Her mother and father were out there. They really had come to the auction. How proud they would be of her tonight. And how glad she was that Henry had come along with them. Victoria must have stayed at home to baby-sit.

The clapping was still going on! Sue Ellen looked back at the members of her class grouped around her on the stage. They certainly did look as if they were working hard. Tod was standing right behind Sue Ellen. He was wearing his cooking apron and a chef's

hat that Mrs. Winter had brought in. He was holding
a big bowl and stirring around and around with a
wooden spoon. Sue Ellen thought he looked just like
the cooks in the ads on television. He was grinning
from ear to ear and looking out into the audience. Sue
Ellen knew he was trying to find his mother in the sea
of faces.

Jenny was on the floor beside Sue Ellen pretending
to paint her bright red box. She was looking out into
the audience, too. Mrs. Briggs was going to be a
helper during the auction and Jenny saw her standing
in a side aisle. Jenny waved her brush and called out,
"Hi, Mummy." Then she glanced quickly over at
Miss Kelly, put her hand over her own mouth and
shook her head as if she were scolding herself for what
she had done. There was a ripple of good-natured
laughter from the audience.

Sue Ellen thought that Ruth and the older girls
looked just right gathered around the kitchen table.
They were wearing their pretty aprons and pretending
to roll out dough and cut out cookies. The big boys
and Patrick were grouped around the work bench, pretending to hammer and saw and sandpaper. Sheri was
sitting near them. She really was making another pot-
holder.

When the audience finally stopped clapping, every-

thing was quiet. For just a minute Sue Ellen was afraid
that someone had forgotten what to do next. Then
Father Tom, who was sitting near the back of the stage,
strummed softly once or twice on his guitar. That reminded Jenny! She looked over at Miss Kelly, got up
off the floor, and said, "Should I say it now, Miss
Kelly?"

Miss Kelly smiled and nodded so Jenny stepped onto
the center of the stage. "Good evening, ladies and
gentlemen," she began. "We're glad you could all come.
We didn't think there would be so many people."
Jenny's speech was different every time she gave it.
"We hope you'll spend a lot of money." There was a
great deal of laughter from the audience. "It's all right
to say that, isn't it, Miss Kelly? We do want them to
spend a lot of money, don't we? We've worked *so*
hard." Again Miss Kelly nodded. "Now we're going
to sing our first song, 'Kumbaya.' " Her speech finished, Jenny bowed and stepped back near Sue Ellen
and Tod. There was lots of clapping for Jenny.

The words that the class sang were not the regular
ones. Father Tom had explained that you don't always
have to sing the same words of a folk song. They can
be changed to fit the needs and feelings of the people
who are singing. He had helped the class make up
their own words especially for the auction. They went
like this:

Someone's selling, Lord, Kumbaya,
Someone's selling, Lord, Kumbaya,
Someone's selling, Lord, Kumbaya,
Oh Lordie, won't you Kumbaya.

Someone's buying, Lord, Kumbaya,
Someone's buying, Lord, Kumbaya,
Someone's buying, Lord, Kumbaya,
Oh Lordie, won't you Kumbaya.

There was more clapping when the song ended. Sue Ellen was so happy that her father and mother were having a chance to see and hear her class doing things together. Last year Sue Ellen had not wanted them to know about anything that happened at school. But this year was different. Perhaps after tonight her mother would understand better why Sue Ellen never wanted to miss a single day of school.

Now it was Patrick's turn to say something. He came forward shyly. He stood very straight and still. Sue Ellen was nervous for Patrick. He had not wanted to be an announcer. The audience waited patiently until he was ready to begin. Then, in a voice that was much too small for the big hall, he said: "Good evening, ladies and gentlemen. Our next song is going to be, 'Rock-a-my Soul.' We will sing it twice. We want everyone to sing it with us the second time." Patrick

bowed stiffly and went back to his place as the audience
clapped for him.

Sue Ellen breathed a sigh of relief that Patrick had
gotten through his part so well, even though he spoke
too softly. She just hoped that the people knew they
were supposed to join in the singing the second time.
Father Tom strummed a chord and the singing began.
It was one of Sue Ellen's favorite songs. The way they
sang it with Father Tom they almost acted it out. They
swayed back and forth as if they were rocking on the
first verse, and then they reached up high, crouched
down low and stretched their arms out wide on the
second verse.

> *Rock-a-my Soul in the bosom of Abraham,*
> *Rock-a-my Soul in the bosom of Abraham,*
> *Rock-a-my Soul in the bosom of Abraham,*
>   *Oh, rock-a-my Soul.*

> *So high you can't get over it,*
> *So low you can't get under it,*
> *So wide you can't get around it,*
>   *Oh, rock-a-my Soul.*

When it came time for the audience to join in, Sue
Ellen heard Mrs. Winter and Miss Foster start to sing
very loudly somewhere out in the big hall. In just a

minute other voices joined in and soon the whole hall rang with the words of the old song. Sue Ellen had discovered Tommy Stroud and his big brother Andy sitting in the front row. Tommy was singing lustily. He didn't seem to think these were junky songs! The audience had a wonderful time singing and they clapped loudly for themselves when they finished.

When the hall was quiet again the children looked at Miss Kelly. She nodded her head and almost everyone started to leave the stage. Of course Jenny had to go over and make an important comment to Miss Kelly first, but after that she joined the other children going down the stairs at the side of the stage. Each one of the children had a special place to which they were supposed to go.

Sue Ellen, Jenny, and Sheri were to be stationed at a long table at one side of the hall. It was covered with cakes, pies, cookies and potholders. When Miss Kelly called them, they were to bring these things up onto the stage to be sold. Polly and Mrs. Cohen, the principal's wife, would be helping them. Tod and Patrick were in charge of the other long table at the other side of the hall. This table held the bird houses, bird feeders, and boot jacks, as well as the guppies and mice. The class had decided that since it was so near the end of the year, they would try to sell all their "livestock" before summer vacation. Mr. Cohen and Mr. Flannigan were ready to help Tod and Patrick take the things from their table up onto the stage when Miss Kelly was ready for them.

Ruth took her place with Polly's mother at a little table just in front of the stage. There was an adding machine and a money box on the table. Mrs. Smith and Ruth were going to keep track of all the money that came in during the evening. This was a very important job.

The three older girls went down and stood in the three aisles. Over their cooking aprons they had now put on carpenters' aprons with a row of little pockets across the front. Instead of having nails of various sizes in the pockets, they had different kinds of money in them. In the first pocket there were four one-dollar bills; in the second, two fifty-cent pieces; in the third, four quarters; and in the last pocket, ten dimes, ten nickels, and ten pennies.

Before the afternoon rehearsal the three girls had gone to the bank with Miss Foster and withdrawn money from the class account. Their job at the auction was to take the money and make change for the people who bought things. The money in their aprons was for making change. Miss Foster, Mrs. Briggs, and Mrs. Carter, the printer's wife, were going to work with the three girls. The girls had practiced making change for weeks and weeks. Doreen told Sue Ellen that she didn't

mind doing that kind of arithmetic, although usually
she hated number work. During the auction, whenever
the girls felt their apron pockets getting too full, they
were supposed to go over to the table where Ruth and
Mrs. Smith were and give them some of their money.

The three older boys were the only members of the
class to remain on the stage. Their job was to help
Father Tom bring forward the things on the stage to
be auctioned off by Miss Kelly. She was going to be
the auctioneer. Sue Ellen wished she was going to be
up on the stage all evening in front of all the people,
but she wasn't.

When Miss Kelly could see that all the children had
taken their places, she stepped to the center of the
stage. "Good evening, ladies and gentlemen," she began. Every speech so far had begun with these words
so she decided to begin hers that way, too! "We certainly are glad to have so many of you here tonight. As
Jenny said, the class has worked very, very hard and
we hope you are here to spend lots and lots of money.
We want to thank everyone who has come, everyone
who has contributed things to sell, and everyone who is
about to spend generously for a good cause." Again
the people clapped.

"Now," said Miss Kelly turning to the big boys and
Father Tom, "if you'll bring the kitchen table forward,
I'll use that as my auction block and we'll begin." Miss

Kelly picked up the wooden mallet that she was going to use for her auctioneer's hammer.

The first thing that was handed to Miss Kelly was a bright red chair that Tod had sanded and painted. Miss Kelly put the chair up on the table in front of her. "I have here a beautiful red kitchen chair painted by Tod Swan. Who will start the bidding on this fine chair with a dollar bill?"

"One dollar!" shouted Father Tom from the back of the stage. He had been planning to buy that red chair ever since the first day he had seen it in Miss Kelly's room. Sue Ellen hoped Father Tom was going to get it.

"Two dollars!" shouted Andy Stroud from the front of the hall.

"Three dollars!" came from the back of the hall.

"Three-fifty," shouted a new voice over at one side.

"Four dollars," said Father Tom with determination.

"Four dollars and fifty cents," from the back of the hall again.

"Five dollars," came from Father Tom.

No one said anything for a minute. Oh, how Sue Ellen hoped Father Tom was going to get it! So did Miss Kelly. She decided not to wait any longer. "I have five dollars, five dollars . . ." and then she added quickly, "and that is enough to pay for this nice red

chair. Going, going, gone!" Down came her wooden
mallet on the table. "Sold to our friend, Father Tom,
for five dollars."

Everyone cheered and Tommy Stroud whistled be-
cause the auction was off to such a good start. Sue
Ellen was happy that Father Tom had gotten his chair.
After that the auction moved right along.

There were chairs and tables, dishes and vases,
kitchen utensils, mirrors and pictures, toys and books.
There was, Miss Kelly said, something for everyone
and everyone for something. Sue Ellen had never seen
so much money spent in her life. The big girls had to
go over to Ruth and Mrs. Smith and empty the money
out of their apron pockets over and over again. The
adding machine kept rattling off numbers all evening
long.

Tommy Stroud and his brother Andy were rapidly
disappearing from view behind all the things they were
buying. Sue Ellen knew that the Stroud boys had an
"Odds and Ends" shop in their barn over in Morristown. They were stocking up on supplies to sell during
the summer. Miss Kelly soon found that when she
couldn't sell something to anyone else, she could always
sell it to Tommy and Andy. She told them that she
was certainly glad they had come to the auction.

Sue Ellen nearly exploded with happiness when she
heard her father bid two dollars for the blue stool she

had sanded and painted. "Sold!" announced Miss Kelly, pouncing on Mr. Stokley's bid before anyone could bid higher. She was delighted that it was going to Sue Ellen's own family.

When Jenny's box came up for sale, Jenny left her place on the floor and walked importantly up onto the stage. She spoke right up. This speech had not been planned. "Come on now, everyone, I want someone to bid a lot of money for this box. I worked hard smoothing it and painting it." The audience had gotten to know Jenny during the evening and they all liked her. Jenny was very pleased when Mr. Cohen bought the box and announced to everyone that it would be placed in the front hall of the elementary school as headquarters for the Lost and Found.

Sue Ellen and Tod carried their own cakes up onto the stage while Miss Kelly auctioned them off. She introduced them as the two youngest cooks in the class. Henry bought Sue Ellen's cake and he paid for it with his own money. He had worked at Petrys' farm every day after school all week to earn the money. Tod's mother bought his cake.

Miss Kelly had discovered, as the auction went along, that every single member of her class had someone there: either a mother or a father or a grandmother. It was the first time that many of these parents had been inside of a school for anything pleasant. Most of them

had come at some time to talk with the teachers or the principals about the problems their children were having. But tonight was different; tonight they were proud and happy parents.

For the final few minutes of the auction, Miss Kelly invited Jenny, Sheri, Patrick, Tod, and Sue Ellen to come up onto the stage with her to auction off the few remaining things. It was just nine o'clock when Sue Ellen held up the last thing to be sold, a rather ugly brown vase. Miss Kelly bought it herself.

"I've got to have something besides a sore throat to show for this evening," she said. "And now, if all the members of my class will come up on the stage, we'll join hands and sing our final song with Father Tom, 'He's Got the Whole World in His Hands.' After that we would like everyone to be our guests for punch and cookies prepared and donated by Mrs. Smith's Home Economics class. Thank you, one and all."

Before the singing began, Mrs. Smith ran up onto the stage. She was waving a long, long piece of paper that she had just pulled out of her adding machine. "I think everyone here will be thrilled to know that this auction has raised $346.50! Let's give three cheers for Miss Kelly and her hard-working class. Hip-hip-hooray! Hip-hip-hooray! Hip-hip-hooray!"

Then Father Tom strummed a few chords and in a minute the auditorium resounded with verse after verse of the folk song, right through to the last verse, "He's got everybody here in His hands."

As Sue Ellen stood singing and swaying to the music, holding Sheri by one hand and Ruth by the other, surrounded by the rest of the class, their families and their friends, she felt herself a part of one great big family. Sue Ellen was happier than she had ever been in her whole life — and tireder too.

12

Things Can Only Get Better

"Get up, Sue Ellen! Come! Get up!" It was Henry trying to wake Sue Ellen up. "The bus will be here soon. You'd better hurry. You sure don't want to miss the bus today."

Sue Ellen rubbed her eyes. Today? Oh no! She mustn't miss the bus today. This was the day that the class was going to visit The Pet Farm. And besides, it was her birthday! She was going to be nine years old today.

Sue Ellen sat up in bed. It felt strange not to have Barbara in bed next to her. The house seemed so empty. Ma was in the hospital, and Barbara, Scott, and Martha were being taken care of by the neighbors. Scott was at the Carlsons' farm, and Barbara and Martha were further along the road at the Hardings'. The neighbors all said they were glad to help out. When Ma was at home she didn't want them helping; "interfering," she called it.

Victoria, Henry, and Sue Ellen were taking care of

themselves after school. Their father was at home at night, but of course he had left for work long ago. Mrs. Smith and Mrs. Winter had brought in several meals, and Polly and Mrs. Smith had taken a load of wash to the laundromat. Polly and Sue Ellen had done the ironing at Polly's house.

Sue Ellen hurried to find clean clothes to put on. She rummaged through the pink plastic wash basket that she and Polly had brought home full of clean, ironed clothes. All the girls had decided to wear shorts on the field trip. Miss Kelly and Miss Foster were going to wear slacks. Most of the things in the basket were pretty mussy now since Victoria and Henry had gone through them looking for their clothes. The shorts and blouse that Sue Ellen finally put on were clean but wrinkled.

Victoria was doing her hair at the sink. Sue Ellen wanted to wash so she slipped in at one corner. Usually her sister gave her a slap when she did that, but today Victoria moved over and let Sue Ellen have a little space in which to wash. Victoria had been nicer to Sue Ellen lately, ever since Polly had taken her to visit Miss Kelly's class one day shortly after the auction. Victoria was going to Parkville to junior high next year, and so Polly had taken her over to visit the seventh grade, too.

Sue Ellen didn't do a very good job of washing herself. She was too excited and in too much of a hurry. When she tried to comb her hair it was so snarled she couldn't get the comb through without hurting, so she just patted it down instead. She looked in the refrigerator and took out an orange. She loved oranges. They never used to have them, but now that Mrs. Winter took Mrs. Stokley shopping occasionally, they sometimes had fresh fruit in the refrigerator.

"You don't have time to eat that orange, Sue Ellen," warned Henry. "You'd better eat some oatmeal. I made it and it's good."

Although she didn't want to, Sue Ellen put the orange back, put some oatmeal in a bowl, and poured milk over it. She put on lots and lots of sugar. She liked cold cereal better than hot, but she ate the oatmeal to please Henry. As she sat eating, she thought about her birthday. No one said anything about it. They didn't remember birthdays in her family. But Miss Kelly knew about it. They were going to have a picnic birthday party for Sue Ellen at The Pet Farm.

As usual, Sue Ellen and Henry were outside before Victoria. While they stood waiting for the bus Henry said: "Ma's coming home tomorrow."

"I know," said Sue Ellen. "Is she all better?"

"I guess so," said Henry. "I sure hope so. She'll be surprised at the new stove, won't she? I wonder if she'll like it or if she'll be mad?"

Father Tom had come up to the house with an electrician at the beginning of the week and helped do the wiring for the stove. Mr. and Mrs. Smith and Mr. Stokley had brought the stove over the night before last in Mr. Smith's pickup truck. Mrs. Smith had shown Mr. Stokley, Victoria, Henry, and Sue Ellen how it worked. Victoria was surprised to find out how much Sue Ellen already knew about cooking. Victoria told Sue Ellen that she was glad she was going to be having Home Ec next year with Mrs. Smith.

Sue Ellen had heard Father Tom talking to her father about putting aside a little money each week for a hot water heater. Mr. Stokley didn't like banks, so Father Tom offered to keep the money for him. Sue Ellen hoped her father would do it, but after Father Tom had left she heard her father tell Henry that he wasn't going to have other people telling him how to spend his money. He said he worked hard all week for his money and he'd spend it the way he wanted to. Sue Ellen felt mixed up. When she listened to Father Tom she agreed with him, but when she listened to her father she agreed with him.

"Here comes the bus!" shouted Henry. "Victoria! Victoria!" The bus made more noise than Henry, but by the time Mr. Washington had turned it around Victoria, as usual, was flying out the back door.

As they drove past Carlsons' Sandy came out and

barked. Sue Ellen looked for Scott but she couldn't see
him any place outside. Probably he was still asleep.
She wished she could see him. Yesterday after school
she and Henry had walked down to see him. He was
all dressed up in clean clothes and he looked so cute!

Mrs. Harding had Barbara and Martha all fixed up
too. Every afternoon Mrs. Harding brought Martha
and Barbara out to meet the bus, and every morning
when the little Harding girl got on the bus she sat with
Sue Ellen and told her all the latest news about Barbara and Martha. She said Martha was learning new
words every day. Sue Ellen was glad Martha was getting all those good meals at the Hardings'. She was
beginning to have some pink in her cheeks, too.

One day after school, Henry and Sue Ellen got off
the bus at Hardings' so they could visit their two little
sisters. Mrs. Harding invited them to supper and Mr.
Harding drove them home. Mrs. Harding told Sue
Ellen and Henry that it was fun for her to have children at home during the day again. She said that she
had never seen two children who were nicer to each
other than Barbara and Martha.

Polly Smith got on the bus at the Center. She sat
down beside Sue Ellen. Polly was going to spend the
entire day with Miss Kelly's class at The Pet Farm.
She was wearing shorts and she was carrying a box and
a picnic basket.

"Happy birthday, Sue Ellen," said Polly. "Aren't you glad it's such a beautiful day for our trip and for your birthday party? I was afraid it might rain." As Polly spoke she looked at Sue Ellen. She had to admit she was disappointed at the way Sue Ellen looked. Polly had spent a lot of time getting the basket of clothes washed and ironed so that Sue Ellen would be sure to have a clean outfit for today's trip. Now, instead of looking neat and clean, Sue Ellen looked quite messy.

Polly sighed. One day recently she had confessed to Miss Kelly that trying to do things for the Stokleys was pretty discouraging. Miss Kelly had sat Polly right down to talk about it. "After all, Polly," Miss Kelly had said, "Rome wasn't built in a day. Helping people grow and learn takes time, lots of time. The Stokleys were having a hard time years before you and I knew them. They'll never have an easy time. Just because some of us are trying to help them now doesn't mean things are going to be different overnight. And anyway, we have no right to try to make them just like us. People are different. I do think we can try to see to it that the children get the right kinds of food to eat and are kept warm and relatively clean. We'll just have to hope that Mrs. Stokley is going to feel more like pitching in when she comes home from the hospital and has a few necessities to work with, like a decent stove and hot water. And if she doesn't, we aren't going to throw up our hands and quit. We'll just keep on trying to teach Sue Ellen and the other children to do as much for themselves as they can."

Remembering this conversation with Miss Kelly, Polly decided not to let discouraging thoughts spoil her whole day. "We're going to have fun today, Sue Ellen. I've never been to The Pet Farm but loads of my friends have. They all say it's a wonderful place. What do you want to see most?"

"I want to see the horse," said Sue Ellen. "Miss Kelly said I might even get to ride the horse. I hope so."

"I want to see the eggs hatching in the incubator," said Polly. "We had an incubator one year in our kitchen."

"What do you have in the box and the basket, Polly?" asked Sue Ellen.

"Oh, just a few surprises that Mother and I made for today," said Polly. "Nothing you'd be interested in." Both Polly and Sue Ellen laughed. They both knew that the box had a birthday present and the basket had a birthday cake for Sue Ellen.

Since the class was going to The Pet Farm in Mr. Washington's bus, Polly and Sue Ellen stayed in their seats when they got to Parkville. Money from the auction was paying for the bus and the picnic lunch. The largest part of the auction money was going to be used to send some of the children to camp during the summer. Sue Ellen would be going to camp for two weeks.

At Parkville the rest of the class climbed aboard the bus. After them came the friends of the class who had helped with the auction: Mrs. Winter, Mrs. Briggs, Mr. Flannigan, and Father Tom. Everyone was carrying something: picnic baskets, or thermos jugs, or suspicious looking packages tied up in birthday wrappings.

The Pet Farm was twenty-five miles away. To the children it seemed much further than that. They had hardly left the center of Parkville when Jenny began to ask: "Are we nearly there?" Fortunately, Father Tom had brought along his guitar and the class sang all the songs they knew.

They sang verse after verse of "Old MacDonald Had a Farm," as Miss Kelly named the animals they would be seeing at The Pet Farm. They sang verses about cows, horses, pigs, rabbits, lambs, goats, chickens, turkeys, geese, ducks, and something called a burro. Sue Ellen wondered what a burro was. They sang "Happy Birthday" to Sue Ellen, too, but Polly said it didn't really count until lunch time.

When the bus reached The Pet Farm, Mr. Wolf, who owned the farm, came out to the bus to meet them. He asked everyone to sit down on the grass while he told them about his farm and his animals. He explained how he had started his farm so that children who did not have animals of their own could enjoy his with him. As he finished he said: "All of the animals here are tame and friendly. They won't hurt anyone. But I want them to stay that way. So please don't run after them or tease them. They want to get to know you as much as you want to get to know them. Just give them a little time. Now have fun and if you have any questions look around for me and I'll try to answer them."

Sue Ellen knew right off that she was going to like The Pet Farm. There were things she wanted to do in whatever direction she looked. First she sat down and held a baby rabbit. Then she helped Sheri give a baby lamb a bottle. She watched Jenny and Ruth help Mr. Wolf milk a goat. She followed the big boys up into the woods to see the pet raccoon. She walked down to the duck pond with the big girls and fed the ducks pieces of stale bread.

About halfway through the morning Miss Kelly was surprised to meet Sue Ellen walking around the farm looking very glum. "What in the world is the matter with the Happy Birthday Girl?" asked Miss Kelly. "You look as if you wanted to go home."

"I can't find the horse!" said Sue Ellen. "You said there would be a horse and there ain't."

"Oh, but there is a horse," said Miss Kelly. "I saw her myself the last time I was here. Let's ask Mr. Wolf where she is."

When they found Mr. Wolf he explained that the horse had had a baby in the night and the mother and baby colt were being kept away from visitors for a few days. "I do plan to let you all take one peek at them before you go home. But I know something you'd like almost as well as a horse," added Mr. Wolf. "That's my burro, Jessie. Come on, I'll show her to you."

Sue Ellen's face lighted up as she skipped along between Miss Kelly and Mr. Wolf. They found the burro standing at the far end of the meadow in the shade of an old apple tree. Sue Ellen discovered that a burro was a small gray animal that looked like a donkey with long hair. Mr. Wolf gave Jessie a pat. Then he turned and picked Sue Ellen up and sat her down on the burro's broad back.

The burro didn't seem as surprised as Sue Ellen. Jessie just looked around once to see who was there, then she lowered her head, bit off a generous mouthful of grass and began to chew. Apparently she was quite used to having Mr. Wolf put unexpected riders on her back.

At first Sue Ellen was frightened. She clutched the burro's rough hair with both of her hands. But gradually, when Jessie did nothing but crop the grass in

front of her, Sue Ellen loosened her hold. She even gave the burro a pat with one hand. Still nothing startling happened, and Sue Ellen was seriously thinking of giving the burro a kick to make her move the way she had seen cowboys do on television. But instead of Sue Ellen doing the kicking, the burro's side gave Sue Ellen a kick! A very surprised little girl grabbed hold of the burro's long hair with two hands again.

"What was that?" asked Sue Ellen, looking terrified.

Mr. Wolf grinned. He had seen what happened. "That was the baby inside of Jessie saying hello. Jessie's going to have a baby in about a week, too. But she doesn't mind you on her back. You're as light as a feather. Don't worry! That baby of hers won't be able to kick you off either. Stay on as long as you want, and when you've sat long enough just slide off. I have to go. I promised Tod that he could help me feed the pig," and Mr. Wolf went off, leaving Sue Ellen and Miss Kelly with the burro.

After a few more minutes of just sitting and no more kicks from baby burro, Sue Ellen asked Miss Kelly a question. "Where's this burro going to get her baby?"

"It's growing inside of her body," explained Miss Kelly. "When the baby burro is ready to be born it will come out of Jessie's body the way the baby colt came out of the mother horse's body, and just the way our baby mice came out of their mother's body."

"Miss Kelly," said Sue Ellen. She had thought of something that had been worrying her. It was something Victoria had said this week. "Is my mother going to bring us home a new baby when she comes tomorrow? Victoria said that every time Ma goes to the hospital she gets us a baby and probably she'd bring one home tomorrow. We don't got no more beds at our house."

At first Miss Kelly didn't say anything. She just went on scratching behind the burro's ears. Jessie turned her head once to let Miss Kelly know that she was scratching in exactly the right spot. Then Miss Kelly said, "No, Sue Ellen, your mother isn't going to bring any more babies home. She's just going to bring herself home tomorrow. And the doctor says that she ought to be feeling a whole lot better. I really think that things can only get better at your house from now on. As for you, Mrs. Jessie, that's all the scratching you're going to get from me for a while. Why don't you slide down now, Sue Ellen, and we'll go into the barn. I want to see what's going on in there today."

Sue Ellen slid down off the burro's back by herself and she and Miss Kelly went into the big red barn. It was divided into several small rooms. They found Polly and Patrick in one of the rooms watching the eggs in an incubator in the center of a low table. The incubator looked like a big glass bubble with eight eggs inside of it. Four of the eggs just looked like regular eggs. Two had little holes cracked in them, and two others were cracked almost all the way around.

"Watch, Sue Ellen," said Polly as Miss Kelly and Sue Ellen came over and stood by the incubator. "Do you see that brown egg near the edge? The one that is most cracked? Patrick and I have been watching that one ever since we came in here and we think that chick is going to be the first one to get out of his shell."

"You can even see his beak," whispered Patrick. "That's what he breaks the shell with. You watch him, Sue Ellen."

Patrick, Polly, Miss Kelly, and Sue Ellen watched as the chick inside the shell suddenly lifted up his head and began tap, tap, tapping at the cracked edge of the shell. He managed to break off another tiny piece of the shell before he collapsed back down inside the unbroken section.

"Oh, dear," sighed Polly, after watching the little chick make three more heroic attempts to break down the doors of his prison, "I wish I could reach in there and break the shell open for him. It looks like such hard work for that poor little thing. But it wouldn't be hard work for me at all."

"I wish I could help, too," said Sue Ellen. "I could smash it open easy."

Miss Kelly put an arm around Polly and another

around Sue Ellen. "That's one thing no one can do for anyone else," she said. "Everything alive — chickens, birds, horses, burros, and even people — every living thing has to do its own being born, and its own growing up, too. No one else can do it for them."

"But couldn't we just help a little?" asked Sue Ellen.

"Mr. Wolf has done all the helping that should be done by putting the eggs in the incubator at just the right temperature with just the right amount of moisture in the air. The rest is up to the chickens in the eggs. That little chick has to make the big push and get himself out," explained Miss Kelly.

As Miss Kelly spoke, the little chick in the partly hatched brown egg lifted his wobbly, wet head again. He seemed to be gathering up all the strength he had left in his fragile body. Then, down came the little beak-hammer on the cracked edge of the shell; and down it came again, and again, and again. And as the children and Miss Kelly watched, the two halves of the shell fell apart and the new-born chick was standing completely free of the shell. And then, exhausted, he fell over in a panting, wet heap.

"He's borned himself," whispered Patrick. "He did it."

"Is he dead?" asked Sue Ellen.

"No, he's alive!" said Miss Kelly. "Born on your birthday, too."

"That's the most wonderful thing I ever saw," exclaimed Polly.

"I'm all tired out just from watching him," said Miss Kelly. "Now I hope he takes a good long rest before he starts in on walking lessons."

Sue Ellen suddenly remembered her new friend, Jessie the burro, down in the field, munching grass. "I'm going to go see Jessie again," said Sue Ellen. "See you later," and she started to skip out of the barn.

"Better be thinking about where you would like us to have your birthday picnic, Sue Ellen," Miss Kelly called after her. "We'll be taking the baskets out of the bus soon."

"I'd like to eat down near Jessie," Sue Ellen called back. "It's nice down there."

Sue Ellen was humming to herself as she skipped along. She felt good. She'd sat on a burro. The baby chick had gotten born. She was going to camp for two weeks this summer. Her mother was coming home tomorrow. Miss Kelly had said that things could only get better at her house. Maybe Victoria would help her make a Crazy Cake in the new stove before Ma got home. She still had the recipe that Polly had written on the cardboard for the auction.

As Sue Ellen skipped along she noticed the big sign over the barn. It said: THE PET FARM. Sue Ellen realized she had read it herself. No one else had read it for her. She was doing some hard things by herself and they weren't hard any more. She was doing her own growing up. She had to. Everybody does.

Sue Ellen began to sing out loud.

Happy Birthday to you.
Happy Birthday to you,
Happy Birthday, Sue Ellen,
Happy Birthday to — me.